To the loving memory of

Crystal, my little sister, the pain of your death changed my life. The memory of your life rescued me.

Crystal Lynn Kenney
(1963-1976)

Note for Librarians: a cataloguing record for this book that includes Dewey Classification and US Library of Congress numbers is available from the National Library of Canada. The complete cataloguing record can be obtained from the National Library's online database at: www.nlc-bnc.ca/amicus/index-e.html

ISBN 14120-2483-8

TRAFFORD

This book was published on-demand in cooperation with Trafford Publishing.
On-demand publishing is a unique process and service of making a book available for retail sale to the public taking advantage of on-demand manufacturing and Internet marketing. On-demand publishing includes promotions, retail sales, manufacturing, order fulfilment, accounting and collecting royalties on behalf of the author.

Suite 6E, 2333 Government St., Victoria, B.C. V8T 4P4, CANADA

Phone 250-383-6864	Toll-free 1-888-232-4444 (Canada & US)
Fax 250-383-6804	E-mail sales@trafford.com
Web site www.trafford.com	TRAFFORD PUBLISHING IS A DIVISION OF TRAFFORD HOLDINGS LTD.
Trafford Catalogue #04-0311	www.trafford.com/robots/04-0311.html

10 9 8 7 6 5 4 3

Chapter One - Sunday
"And God said, let there be light"

PREACHERS FORGET ALL THOSE THINGS they don't want to remember, and remember everything they don't want to forget. It's all about the memory. Old scars left to whither in the deep recesses of the subconscious. Fantasies left unexplored by fear. Thoughts rejected due to the glare of a suspicious member. All eyes are on the preacher. You never know who's watching.

Simon had lived a life in solitude. Always present, yet always absent. His body walked through the crowd with confidence, yet his mind was lost in the deep weeds of memory. He couldn't say what he felt. He couldn't feel. Pain, sorrow, rejection, anger, frustration, hostility, lust, passion, irritation, depression—emotions felt by those in need of the resolve found in the church, yet denied the preacher.

How could he stop from being angry? The envy had consumed him. Watching so many testify of the love, kindness, and forgiveness of an awesome God left him resentful of the people he ministered to. They didn't hesitate to cry. They were free to shout.

They could confess their wrongdoings in the presence of the people without fear of retaliation and rejection. Not so for the preacher.

The people all saw him coming because it was worship time. It was time for sitting in the pews in the church. It was time to hear the old songs. These sitters had been waiting all week. The toil of the week had brewed deep malice. They needed to hear a word from God. All eyes were on Simon. Is there a word from the Lord this morning?

Seeing the people as he made his way to the pulpit reminded him of the envy he had stored up. He remembered the burning statements and questions. He remembered the mass cruelty. The words walking without masters. They smiled and shouted. They praised God, but these saints had bitten more than once. The venom from their bite had poisoned the loving community.

Simon moved to North Carolina to teach at Duke University in Durham. He came after completing his Ph.D. in Theology at Princeton Theological Seminary. He entered the Ph.D. program after serving two others churches. He had become tired from the demands of ministering to Church folks. Somehow he got suckered into going back into the parish. Durham was a great place to live. It was a terrible place to serve a church.

Durham was one of the few cities in the country that lacked a history of strong black church leadership. Most of the leaders came from the business community. Because of this, persons in ministry took a back seat in developing a vision for the black community. Simon had attempted to change that legacy. It didn't work.

"What he doing coming back here after what he put us through? Where's his wife and children? Why don't he just resign? He can't even control his

own household. Where's the woman he's sleeping with? I hear he's on drugs. He thinks he better than us."

He felt their questions. When he got in the pulpit he turned his face on the podium and spoke. "If the Lord's been good to ya, say Amen, somebody." The people scrambled a noisy "Amen" and left their mouths wide open and their ears waiting for gossip bait. His speech was pleasant, but his heart was black and blue from the battle.

The choir sang. The groove of the band diverted attention away from the tears Simon sucked back. Tears would be used as a weapon against his strength. They hoped and prayed that he would fall to their level one day. He sat and sucked.

Deacon Andrews opened his mouth, "Amen." He didn't know what else to say. The sound of his voice had become a common fixture at the Shady Grove Church. He had ruled for three decades. Deacon Andrews had baptized many good pastors into the reality of Christian duty. Well intentioned, God loving and God fearing men had left broken and bruised.

Andrews was the gatekeeper. His task was to keep the pastor in place—by any means necessary. The church belonged to the people, and any pastor who forgot that was stoned. He didn't care if the people left. His family helped build the church. Everyone knew the story. His grandfather bought the land, and motivated members to build the church on the current site. Deacon Andrews, then only 7, helped build the church.

Simon took a quick glimpse at Deacon Andrews. He watched him praise God. He listened to his Amens and thank you Jesuses. What did it all mean? He sucked back tears-again. "You mean

asshole," Simon whispered to himself as he prepared to preach. There was no doubt about it, Simon didn't like Andrews, and Andrews didn't like Simon. The old cat and mouse game was beginning to show. The members knew the truth.

"There is a word from the Lord," Simon began. "It's a fresh word, an inspired word. It's a word that cuts like a two edged sword."

"Amen," the chants could be heard as the members waited for a spiritual eruption.

"Turn to Daniel, Chapter 6, verse 19-20," the sound of pages filled the air. "If you have it say Amen. If you don't, say wait preacher."

The laughter broke the ice. Simon needed laughter to help him forget how insane things were. Preaching had become a dreaded task.

"At the first light of dawn, the king got up and hurried to the lion's den. When he came near the den, he called to Daniel in an anguished voice, 'Daniel, servant of the living God, has your God, whom you serve continually, been able to rescue you from the lions?'"

"You all know the story of Daniel," it was time for his introduction. "Daniel prayed all day. He prayed all night. He prayed because he had to pray. He found himself at one of those inopportune times of life. Not by his own choosing. Not because of something he had done. Daniel had to pray because the king placed him in a lion's den." Simon turned his back to the congregation to speak to those sitting in the choir stand. He noticed Alice Grant pass a note to Helen Coleman. Passing notes during his sermon had become a common ritual at Shady Grove.

"The oddity of the text is the reason Daniel is placed in the lion's den," Simon continued. "He is placed there not because the king wanted him there.

6

He broke no law that harmed another human. He harmed no one. He didn't get arrested for stealing property. He stole nothing. He didn't get busted for violating another man's woman. He didn't assault anyone. He got arrested for something many folk refuse to do. Daniel got locked up for praying three times a day. He prayed in the morning, giving God thanks for the start of another day. He prayed in the middle of the day, asking for the strength to make it through. He prayed at the end of the day, giving thanks for another day's journey. Three times a day, everyday, Daniel prayed, despite the order handed down by King Darius, he still prayed.

"Daniel did not want to be disobedient. He was the kind of guy that respected authority. But prayed anyhow, because Daniel understood that he could not make it without prayer." Three choir members left the church in the middle of his sermon. This too had become a common disruption. It was their way of letting the people know they weren't happy with the sermon and the messenger.

"He's placed in the lion's den. Why would God allow one of his faithful servants to be locked up for having conversation with the divine? Why didn't God close the ears of those who meddled in Daniel's business so Daniel could continue to do the business of praying to God? How is it, that God would jeopardize the life of one of his best, just because he wanted to pray?" Simon noticed people talking throughout the church. He remembered being told to preach in season and out of season. It was off-season at Shady Grove.

"This text isn't just about Daniel's overcoming the hunger pangs of lions in a den. It's not just about God coming to the rescue of a faithful servant. This is a text that challenges us to pray

even when we're told not to pray. For prayer is the key that unlocks the door. Prayer is the answer to all that perplexes the human soul. This text places Daniel in the middle of a confrontation between God and those who attempt to keep God's people from doing what God says do." Simon took a peek at Deacon Andrews. He sat with his arms crossed and a stern look on his face.

"Now understand, Daniel wasn't worried when he went down in the lion's den. The text makes it clear that he was confident that God would make a way somehow. The question for us is why is he so confident? It doesn't make any sense, Daniel being confident in a lion's den. Why no tears? Why no concern for tomorrow? Why no doubt lifted off the pages of this text? How can a man go down into the lion's den without fighting to stay out?

"The first possibility is that Daniel had confidence because he'd been praying. He prayed three times a day, every day. He didn't wait until things got out of hand to go to God in prayer. He praised God and prayed to God three times a day every day, so when the time came for Daniel to endure the test of his faith, he was prayed up, and knew God would provide.

"What I'm trying to say is the lion's den isn't as grueling if you prayed before the lion den comes your way. Now, let me warn you. Everything may be all right now. The sun shines everyday on your side of the street. The bills are paid, and the home life is the life you prayed for. But don't be surprised if the weeping comes. For life is a series of ups and downs. Today may be your good day, but trouble is on the way, and when it comes, remember, trouble don't last always.

"He was confident. He was at peace because he prayed, three times a day. But not only that. He

8

was confident, he was at peace because he knew, no weapon formed against him would prosper. Even the king didn't want to see him go down. This was not the plan of an evil King. Darius was a good king. This was the plot of evil, jealous administrators of the king. These administrators fought Daniel because Daniel was favored by the king. They wanted to get him out of the way.

"There comes a time in life when people fight against you not because of anything you do, but because of their jealousy toward you. When this comes remember these words, no weapon formed against you will prosper. Daniel knew that this too is in the hands of God. Daniel realized that this weapon would not prosper because the battle never belonged to him. He wasn't fighting against those who fought. They were fighting against God.

"Not only did he know that. Daniel also knew that the Lord would fight his battle, because again, the battle belonged to God. Look at what happens in the text. The men, who sought to harm Daniel, were brought to the king after God spared Daniel. Before they reached the floor of the den, the lions overpowered them and crushed all their bones. Not only that, their wives and children were thrown into the den. I hate to scare anybody, but you need to know that you still reap what you sow."

It was obvious that this sermon made reference to the life of Shady Grove. Week after week Simon did his best to keep the business of the church out of his sermon. The problem was, too much of their business popped up in the word of God.

Preacha' Man

Chapter Two – Monday

"Nobody knows the trouble I've seen"

MONDAY IS ALWAYS THE HARDEST DAY. Sunday takes its toll on those in ministry. Much needed rest escapes those who utter a message of hope to God's people. The demands of the people make it difficult to unwind. Simon was tired. Tired from having preached. Tired of having to smile at those who desired to destroy him. Tired of playing the church game.

The fire of his earlier years had become a distant memory. Lost were the days when he looked forward to doing God's work. Lost was the meaning and purpose of ministry. It no longer made sense. It was a game. Nothing more and nothing less. Simon feared that people would find him out. His gift helped cover his burnout. It was more than burnout. He wondered if he had made a mistake. Maybe what he acknowledged as a call from God wasn't. Maybe he had missed out. It was too late to turn back. There's a special place in Hell for those who walk away from God's work.

The phone rang. Simon looked at the clock. It was too early for a phone call. "Damn, what they want now," he moaned as he reached for the phone on the living room coffee table. His wife was asleep in the bedroom. He didn't want to awake her. The previous night was another battle of words over the women of the church. He couldn't take anymore of her accusations. He could hear her blast, "Is that one of your bitches calling?"

It was 6:30 a.m. Who could it be? "Hello." He tried his best to camouflage his exhaustion. Church members liked thinking their pastor rose early to pray. Simon had stopped praying a long time ago. His cruise control settled in after his first fight at Shady Grove. He was embarrassed to admit that the things he taught others had escaped his own life. There were many excuses for his lack of spiritual discipline. He had the benefit of a theological education, and the advantage of a history of toil. The truth is he knew that his lack placed his ministry in question. He stopped praying because he stopped believing. The work was a job.

"Who is it?" He really didn't care. He only hoped that the news on the other end would not require his getting off the couch.

"It's Deacon Andrews. We been talkin' and we need to talk to you." Simon wasn't surprised. The talk in the streets was that the deacons would push for his resignation.

"Who's we, and when would we like to meet," Simon lashed back. He didn't care how his words would be perceived. It was him against the world. That's how he felt. No matter what he said, the judgment would be the same. He knew that the meeting would be like the lion's den he just preached about.

"The church members been talkin, and they come to us. They say it's time for a change. We need to meet." Andrews' voice raised a few notches. "You free on Thursday?"

Simon couldn't escape the inevitable. "I'm free. I'll be there at 6:30."

What a way to start the morning, Simon thought as he hung up. Yesterday's service wasn't enough to fight off the demons. He had been taught that the secret to success in the black church was good preaching. No matter what happens, if you can preach you'll be able to fight your way out of any controversy. That wasn't enough to satisfy these demons.

The demons at Shady Grove were a special breed. The things that satisfied most churches went unnoticed. The growth in membership and finances didn't matter. The focus on community and inner healing didn't matter. What mattered the most to the old members was maintaining the status quo.

Simon desired the strength to walk away. The thing that kept him at bay was the faces of those who supported him. When he thought of resigning they came to mind. He remembered their tears, their laughter, their words of encouragement, and the change in their lives. He couldn't walk away from them. He stayed put because he needed them. They reminded him of his purpose. He found meaning through them.

He loved most of the people, but the fighting had worn at his soul. All the talk about insignificant matters made him wonder about his faith. If this is the Church, then he didn't want to be a part of it. He knew this wasn't the Church.

"Who was that?" His wife Janet made her way to the living room. Her forehead showed the

sign of rage. Her voice lacked the tenderness he needed.

"Deacon Andrews." He kept his face to the ground. He could no longer stand the look of her face. The love died sometime between the first and second child. Since then the rumors of affairs and close calls had ruined any chances of a happy home.

They were married straight out of high school. Janet suckered Simon into marrying her after she got pregnant. The rumor was the child wasn't his. It didn't matter. He refused to be accused of not taking care of his responsibility. She knew Simon hated her. She knew it was only a matter of time before he walked out the door. The only reason he stayed was fear.

He feared what the people would say. Even more painful was the fear of what he felt. He agonized over trying to reverse the negative images of black men. He heard it everyday. There are more black men in prison than in college. Black men have failed their children. He didn't want to be another statistic. He stayed to prove white people wrong. It was his obligation.

"You lying. Why would he call you this early?" He knew it was coming. Janet was convinced that Simon was having an affair with Bonita. The thought had crossed his mind. Bonita was an older, attractive woman. She had expressed interest in Simon, but he fought the temptation.

"You know it's your bitch," Janet uttered. Last night's conversation started all over again. He didn't need this. He feared striking Janet. The only way to shut her up was to shake her a few times. He didn't need the reminder of past mistakes. Simon needed the support of a loving wife. Instead he was chastised for having a sweet tooth for sexy women.

Janet had reason to fear. Simon had a history of stepping out. He wasn't proud of his past, but the past was the past. It happened 10 years ago. It happened after a series of fights. He was ready to leave, and he would have if the woman had been willing. Her name was Jamaica. Like her name, she was hot, spicy and exotic. She had the perfect body, long hair, and a craving for wild things. While with her he forgot about being holy and pure. He was willing to leave it all for her.

Jamaica didn't want a relationship. She wanted an affair. Simon got caught up, and before he knew it the word was out in the streets. His reputation was tarnished, and Janet lost trust. She never really trusted him, but Jamaica gave her reason not to trust. She lacked Jamaica's looks and moves. She was a Camry and Jamaica was a Porsche.

Janet used her rage to prove herself. After graduating from Rutgers with a degree in psychology, she enrolled at Princeton where she completed her Master in Psychology and PhD in Clinical Psychology. She was smart and capable. She lacked confidence in her marriage, but had the stuff to stand on her own.

"I've got to go," the words came out. He had nowhere to go other than to the office, and working was the last thing on his mind. The people at the church were convinced he was a workaholic. The truth is he went to the office to get away from the noise at home. It was either that or get caught up in activity that would get him in real trouble.

"Don't you walk away from me." Janet had a need to talk. She suspected the worst. The lipstick on Simon's collar, and the cards in his pocket; the

late night phone calls, and the sessions behind closed doors—she couldn't take it anymore.

"Mamma, can you iron my shirt," Chris, the oldest child asked as he walked into the war zone. Simon hated fighting in the presence of the children. He was afraid of what he would do or say. The memories of his father and mother came to mind. His father often struck his mother in the heat of battle. His mother would hit back. He remembered the cursing. He learned things about his mother and father that should be shielded from a child. He didn't want that with his two children. Chris was 16. Carmen was 14.

Many of Simon's problems were connected to his childhood. The recall of past years left him stripped of self-worth. He did his best to keep things in the present. He couldn't face what used to be. The church became his shelter from the memories. A protection from the locked closets of his subconscious. He couldn't go there. He needed to, but it was too much to bear.

•

Innocence is a terrible thing to lose. Once lost you can never get it back. It's especially painful when you lose it without giving it up. It's painful being stripped of your innocence before you're ready to let it go.

Childhood years should be enjoyed. Adults are there to protect children from the loss of innocence. They should shield youth from the vicious venom of the cruel snakes who slither through life in search of youthful victims.

It was springtime. The grass was green, and clovers had already poked their heads between the blades. The birds made music, entertaining all who took time to hear. Springtime in Missouri is a great time. Springtime is the resurrection of a long, cold

winter. New life is found in springtime. It's a time to be glad.

School was over, and as usual Simon made his way home. He lived one mile from the school, and all the black kids in his neighborhood walked home each day. It was an easy walk. The sidewalk down Sexton Road took him to McBaine Street. McBaine took him to Dean Street. He lived at 309 Dean Street. It was a great neighborhood. The Hickmans, Nunnleys, Crums, Coxes, Ratliffs, all made the neighborhood one big family.

Simon felt protected. He knew that the people in the neighborhood cared for him and all the other children in the 'hood. It was a peaceful neighborhood. Everyone was a homeowner. The projects were three blocks away, but Simon's block was like Peyton Place among black folks. These blacks were considered elite in the city. Although struggling, it was understood that his neighborhood was a class above that of other black neighborhoods.

Simon enjoyed the walk home. He usually walked alone. The walk gave him time to get his thoughts together. No one ever told him it wasn't safe to walk home alone. Mamma told him to watch out for strangers, but no one warned him about those close to him.

"Simon you need a ride? It's a long walk." It was a family friend. He was right. It was a long walk home. The black kids were denied the advantages of whites. They rode the bus home. He had to walk. It was a long way to walk for a 5th grader. Simon didn't care. He liked the walk.

"Get in boy." The tone in his voice left young Simon no option but to get in. He was a family friend. He had nothing to fear.

"What you been doing boy," he asked as Simon hopped into his truck.

"Nothin'."

"What your daddy been up to," he uttered as he pulled from the corner in front of the school. He quickly pulled up to the stop sign on the corner of Garth and Sexton. He should have gone straight. He turned right. He's going the wrong way, Simon thought. Maybe he knows a short cut. Maybe he has to stop somewhere first. He kept moving the wrong way.

He kept talking as if nothing was wrong. Simon remained silent. Only nodding when asked a question. Why is he going the wrong way, Simon continued to ponder. Soon they were outside city limits. Simon was scared now. Why are we here? What is he doing?

He pulled down a gravel road. There were trees on both sides of the road. Simon felt panic. Why are we here? He couldn't speak. The man kept talking as if nothing was wrong. Simon wanted to go home.

He stopped the truck. "Boy, I'm gonna teach you how to be a man." There was a mean look in his eyes. "I ain't gonna hurt ya. Just do what I tell ya to do." He unzipped his pants. Simon tried to run, but he stopped him. "Don't run boy. Just do what I say." He grabbed Simon's arm tight as he attempted to open the door. Simon was too far away from home to run. There was no one to hear him shout.

He pulled out his penis. It was black and ugly. "Touch it boy. This is what a man looks like." Simon didn't know what to do. "Touch it boy!" His raised voice was a warning to do what he said. Simon touched his penis. As Simon touched it the limp penis grew in his hand.

"That's what a man looks like. Rub it boy. Rub it up and down." Simon did as he said. Something wasn't right. This couldn't be what men do—could it? Simon wanted to be a man, but this seemed wrong. Simon did as he said hoping it would all end soon. He wanted to go home. He wanted to go outside and play football with his friends.

As Simon rubbed the ugly black thing, the family friend moaned. "Harder boy, rub it harder. Faster, um, ah, um yeh, that's right." Simon did as he said. Soon it got easier. But then it got worse.

"Put it in your mouth!" Simon stopped rubbing. He couldn't believe what he heard.

"No," Simon cried. "Why would he ask me to do that?" Simon whispered. He slapped him across the face.

"Do what I say boy! I told you I'm gonna teach you how to be a man. Don't you want to be a man?"

"Yeah," he answered. What else could he say?

"Put it in your mouth and suck it like a lollipop." He took Simon's head and forced it down to his penis. He forced his penis into Simon's mouth and made him suck it. Like a lollipop. It made him sick. He wanted to throw up, but he couldn't get up. His hand forced Simon's head down. He grabbed Simon's hair and moved it up and down, up and down, up and down.

It lasted for what seemed an eternity. He moaned, "um, ah, yeah boy, that's right, give it to me, give it to me." Then it happened. A white creamy fluid spurted out from the tip of his penis. "Swallow it boy! Swallow it like a man!" Simon had no choice. He did as he said. It tasted like

vomit. It was all over his face. Simon screamed. He wanted to bite him but he couldn't. He was too scared to bite.

"You a man now! You a good cock sucker!" He laughed. Like a mad man he laughed at Simon. "Don't you tell nobody boy! If you tell your daddy or your mamma I will kick your black ass. This between me and you. Nobody else need know how you become a man."

Simon never said a word. The long ride home gave him the strength not to speak. He was too scared that it would happen again.

The past months had been filled with one flashback after another. One bad dream after another. The tears kept coming. He had nowhere to go with those tears. No pastor to tell. No friend to confide in. No place to lay his heavy load. He carried the ache like a martyr. It was his badge of courage. No one knew.

Preaching became his lone oasis from the flashbacks of dicks flying at his face and the sound of rude laughter in his ear. Worship became his sole refuge from the relentless reminder of a kept secret. He had tried to share his pain with Janet. That was a big mistake.

It was after a flashback. He was in the bed shaking like the last leaf on a tree. He was sweating and crying.

"What's wrong," she asked, seemingly concerned.

"You don't want to know," Simon whispered.

"Yes I do. What's wrong with you."

Simon closed his eyes as he remembered that moment. He remembered swallowing his pride.

"I'm having flashbacks." It was out there. He felt the relief. After all those years of holding the pain inside, he finally shared it with another person.

He remembered thinking, maybe this will strengthen our marriage.

"What? Are you remembering, getting high?" she asked. Everyone knew that Simon was a recovering addict. He had hidden his addiction from members of the church for years. He decided that the best way for him to support the men and women of the church who grappled with addiction was to be real about his own struggles.

"No. It's not drugs," he hesitated. "I'm having flashbacks of being sexually abused. It's like I'm reliving it all over again."

Janet looked at him bewildered. What she did next radically changed his marriage. She turned around, left the room, and slammed the door. Finally he had gotten the load off his back. What he got wasn't support. He received rejection.

The remainder of that night was spent processing Janet's response. Maybe she had placed Simon on a pedestal and his news forced him to lower ground. Maybe she couldn't hear his pain because it reminded her of something in her past. Maybe she was disgusted at the thought of someone being with her husband. Simon cried through the night. He needed Janet. Instead of a warm embrace he got a door slammed in his face. He then knew that it was time to end his marriage. He could never love her again. He could never forgive her for refusing to hear him. It was the beginning of the end.

It became difficult for Simon to focus on ministry after that night. Not only was it the beginning of the end of his marriage, it was the beginning of a radical transformation in his life. The problem was finding a place to process the pain. It was expected that he would create a place for others

to come to unwind, unload and reflect, but he lacked a person like himself to make sense of the chaos. Realty would let him cry. The work would let him move past the pain.

•

Simon made it to the office by 9:00 a.m. "Good morning, Pastor," Sophie, his administrative assistant said as he entered her office. He grabbed his messages, and turned to go to his office.

"You too good to speak this morning," Sophie snapped. She knew Simon well. For six years she had served as his assistant. Over the years she had learned to read his mood shifts.

"I'm sorry, Sophie. Good morning." She smiled knowing it would be enough to heal the hurt caused by his neglect. He knew Sophie had an interest in more than a professional relationship. She was dedicated and hard working. Her dedication helped cover her deficiencies. She lacked basic skills needed to do her job. Simon protected her from the criticism because of her commitment to him. That was more important as far as he was concerned.

"What do I have today?"

"Patsy Hughes called. She wants to see you today. I told her I'd get back with her after talking with you."

"Go ahead and schedule her. Do I have anything else?"

"You remember Deacon Stanley's funeral is tomorrow. The family called to finalize things."

"What time is the funeral?"

"1:00"

Simon turned to go his office. Sophie gaped at his butt as he walked away. Unholy thoughts went through her mind. She imagined him kissing her, touching her, undressing her and throwing her

on the desk. What would it be like to make love on her desk?

She wanted to be there for Simon. She hated the way Janet treated him. She didn't appreciate what she had. Sophie could stroke him in the right places. She wanted for him to make the first move. He never did.

His desk was stacked with papers. A reminder of work not done. It was too much to deal with in one day. He thought of throwing the stack into file 13, but feared missing out on an important event.

He took a peek at his carpet. He had asked to have it cleaned three months back. He hated walking into a messy office. He wanted order. He wanted a place that made him glad to be called the pastor of Shady Grove. He was embarrassed when other ministers visited the church.

"Back to work," he whispered to himself. He remembered tomorrow's funeral. Funerals were always tough. The family wanted a reminder of how wonderful their loved one was. In this case Simon had no fond words to share. Deacon Stanley had been the architect behind the movement to have him fired.

It all started the previous year. Rufus, Simon's best friend died on Monday. The word spread throughout the city. Many wondered how Simon would take the loss of Rufus. They were like thunder and lighting. Simon took the loss badly.

Deacon Stanley interrupted a serious crying session. "Brother Pastor, we been thinking. It's time for you to resign. We giving you two weeks to resign or we gonna bring it to the church," he said.

Simon didn't know what to do. He couldn't believe how he was attacked during a vulnerable

moment. He couldn't speak. His only thought was how would Rufus deal with this crap. Two days later Simon was rushed to the hospital. He thought it was a heart attack. It was a stress attack.

"You reap what you sow," Simon murmured. "The Bible says touch not God's anointed." Resentment had gotten the best of Simon. He knew the scriptures that roused the love of enemies. He knew that he was to turn the other cheek and love those who used him. Knowing the scriptures didn't help. He hated Deacon Stanley. He wasn't sad that he was dead. He saw it as God's vindication.

He opened his Bible to find a text for the eulogy. A friend had shared with him a story of a pastor who had to preach the eulogy of a critical deacon. He chuckled as he remembered what the pastor said. He was told the pastor walked to the podium. Looked at the family members. Paused for what seemed to be an eternity and said, "My mother told me, if you don't have anything nice to say, don't say anything." The pastor then turned around and walked back to his seat.

"I could do that," he thought for a brief moment. He knew better. He lacked the personality. At times he wished he had the guts to do something like that. "I've got to think on his good qualities," Simon whispered. "Despite the Hell in that man there was something good. There had to be some good."

He bowed in meditation. What good could be said? He turned to Psalm 46. "That man had a deep faith in God." That was it. "God is our refuge and strength, an ever present help in trouble. Therefore we will not fear, though the earth give way and the mountains fall into the heart of the sea, though the waters roar and foam and the mountains quake with they're surging," he read.

He wrote his thoughts down. In times like these we are reminded our only true refuge is in God. The world changes. We are powerless over nature. The waters roar at their own doing. We can't control that. The mountains quake. We can't stop that. Nations are in an uproar. We wish we could find world peace. Kingdoms come and go. What do we do in times like these? Our only refuge is in God. Deacon Stanley understood that. He would want for us to remember that.

Deacon Stanley was able to see beyond the tempest. It takes the eye of faith to do that. Some people can't see past the storm. Some drown in the waves of life. Others jump ship when the storm clouds roam. Not Deacon Stanley. He had faith. He could see beyond the tempest. He lived this test.

He read some more. "Be still, and know that I am God; I will be exalted among the nations. I will be exalted in the earth." He wrote some more. Deacon understood something we all need to learn. If you want to find God, you have to be still. The text challenges us to be still when the storm comes. Be still when the going is rocky. Be still when nation is against nation and friends war among themselves. Be still when the heat of the day dries up hope and the cold of the night freezes one's desire for a better day. Be still and know that God is God. God is God when you can't feel God. God is God when you don't feel like shouting. God is God no matter what. Just be still.

Simon closed his eyes. He would preach on the importance of being still. That was the message learned in this death. He was satisfied.

There was a knock at the door. "Come in." He hated being interrupted in the middle of sermon preparation.

"Patsy is here to see you." Sophie knew it was a bad time. "Can you see her now?" She hoped he would say no. Pasty was a pretty girl. The type of woman that could steal her man.

"It's okay."

The room changed when Patsy stepped into his office. The perfect shape of her body was enhanced by her dress. She reached over to hug Simon. "Good morning, Pastor."

She smelled great. Her fragrance reminded him of vanilla beans. "How you been, Patsy? I didn't see you at church yesterday."

"You noticed I wasn't here?" She smiled as she sat down. The seat was on the other side of his desk. The distance seemed too close. The door was closed. Simon's heart was pounding

"I noticed because you always sit in the same place. The third pew on my right."

"That's true. I had a family reunion yesterday. I heard you preached a powerful message. I'm sorry I missed it."

"Pray for me. I always need your prayers."

"I'm always praying for you, Pastor. I worry about you. Sometimes I wonder how do you make it."

"God gives me the strength. I have to keep focused on what God would have me do instead of being distracted by what others think."

"I hear you. I just don't know how you do it. That's why I'm here."

"I thank you for your support, Patsy. That means a lot."

"I want to do more than support you, Pastor. I was thinking of how you've been there for me over the years. When I broke up with Gerald you helped me. I thought the world was coming to an end. You helped me see that God protected me from making a

bad mistake. I thought Gerald would be my husband. That devastated me."

"I remember. Look how far God has brought you."

"Yeah, I thank God for that. I'm a different person. I've thought a lot about that, Pastor. There are so many people in this church who've been blessed by what you say. You're never too busy to take the time to listen to what we have to say. But what about you? Who do you go to when you need to let it all out? That made me sad, Pastor. With all the Hell that you're going through around here, who do you have to talk to?"

It was a good question. Simon didn't have a person to go to. "I have God, Patsy. I also have friends across the country who pray with me."

"Who do you have here? Don't you need someone to go to?"

"That would be nice, Patsy. We all need a friend."

"I want to be that person, Pastor. I want to be the person you go to. You can come to me and tell me anything. It all stops here." She reached out to hold his hand. He didn't fight her touch. He wanted her friendship. He wanted more than that. Her voice was seducing him.

"I don't know if that's such a good idea." He was trembling. She could sense his uneasiness.

"Why, Pastor? Because you're attracted to me? I'm attracted to you. I'm tired of fighting what I feel." All cards were on the table. She stood. "It's okay, Pastor. I know how you feel. I know what you need. You need a friend."

She reached out to kiss him. Gently on the cheek. Her eyes gazed deep into his eyes as if in

search for an answer. "I won't hurt you, Pastor. You can trust me." He wanted to believe her.

He peeked at her firm legs. The skirt was short. The legs were brown and long. She noticed his gaze.

"It's okay, Pastor," she kissed again. This time soundly on the lips. "You can have me. I'm here for you." She sat in his lap and took control. "Don't say no. Let me take care of you."

For a moment he let her. He forgot it was the office. He touched her thighs. Slowly he moved up to her panty line. His index finger touched where it feels good. That place that makes women moan. She moaned and moved. "Let me take care of you," gently she whispered in his ear touching his face.

There in his office, surrounded by holy relics, he kissed and touched. Her neck, her lips, her thighs. Their body temperatures increased. It was time to remove linen. The only thing left was to come out of blouse and pants, shirt and skirt, panty and underwear. It was time to kiss down there. He wanted to taste her warm place. The thought of her soft lips kissing his solid organ brought him joy.

There was a knock on the door. Back to reality.

•

Sophie watched Patsy walk out of Simon's office with a smirk on her face. You could feel the sin as it made it's way to the door. Sophie fought back her tears. She lacked Patsy's good looks and nice figure, but she was a better match for the man of God. That's how she felt.

She wondered what happened behind those closed doors. Patsy was long past the breakup with Gerald. Gerald left Patsy in the middle of planning for a June wedding. It took everyone by surprise. Patsy and Gerald were the model couple at Shady

Grove. Gerald was Assistant District Attorney. Patsy worked as a stockbroker. Both made good money. Both had good looks. They were perfect for one another.

When Gerald walked away from every man's dream woman, everyone wanted to know why. Patsy took it personal. The truth of the matters is Patsy was more hurt by being embarrassed than with losing Gerald. She had to pick up the pieces of her life after explaining to the world why she and Gerald weren't getting married.

That was a long time ago. Three years had passed, and Patsy still hadn't dated. Many tried, but her tough exterior left many afraid to come back after being told she was too busy. The only man that caught her attention was Simon. For three years the two met each week to talk. That's a long time to heal. At some point someone needed to put an end to this game.

Many others deserved a chance to speak to the pastor. Sophie had to juggle Simon's schedule each week to accommodate their weekly fix. Each week she fought back the temptation to say to her boss, "Tell that woman to get over it."

She was losing her patience with Simon. She took the job at Shady Grove for one reason — to get her man. She did everything she knew to get his attention. She worked long hours, brought him lunch, wore revealing clothes, spoke in a gentle voice. None of it worked. What man wouldn't want to spend time with a woman like her? She wasn't ugly. No, she didn't have the flair of Patsy. Not many did. But what she possessed was decent looks and a nice personality.

She looked forward to those rare occasions when she and Simon talked about personal matters. The last time was two weeks ago.

"Why aren't you dating, Sophie? I would think there are many men interested in taking you out," he began. "Or are you doing things on the down low?"

"I'm waiting for Mr. Right," she answered. "I don't have no time for no jive man. Most of them only want one thing, and I ain't going there!"

"Excuse me for asking. Sounds like home girl got some issues with the brothers. I ain't mad at you. Brothers don't know how to treat a good woman like you."

He said it. He called her a good woman. He noticed. She hung on those words for days, analyzing his tone, choice of words, eye contact, and placement of hands. "Brothers don't know how to treat a woman like you," became "You're a good woman, and I know how to treat a woman like you."

What did he mean? Has he been thinking about me? Did he notice I've lost weight? She loved everything about him. His face, his voice, his body, the way he dressed, his drive, his commitment—she loved everything.

It's the only reason she took the job. It's the only reason she stayed. She knew of the complaints regarding his service to the church. He'd been accused of being with other women. She knew that was a lie. If he were the womanizer they claimed him to be, he would have made a move on her. Others claimed he was gay. That came mostly from the women in the church who got their feelings hurt when they made a move. Simon was a good man, who dedicated himself to the work of the church to a fault.

She knew that his days at the church could soon end. A meeting was set for Thursday. The deacons had called her to uncover some ammunition for the meeting. They were busy digging up dirt to sling at the meeting. They were playing hardball, and she didn't want to be a part of that game. She was dedicated to Simon. If no one else would stand by his side, she would.

"Pastor, you have a phone call." Sophie didn't recognize the voice of the woman on the phone. "Her name is Jamaica Stephens."

"Thanks, Sophie. I'll take it," Simon replied. Sophie went through the membership roll on the database to find Jamaica's name. It wasn't there. Who is this woman? It was hard enough fighting with Patsy Hughes. All she needed was more competition.

She waited for Simon to get off the phone. She was wearing a new outfit she purchased the previous night. It accented her breast and legs. Sophie was proud of her legs. Dark and smooth. On many occasions she had caught Simon looking at her legs. She hoped this outfit would drive him crazy. Her firm breasts were ready to be stroked by the hands of the holy man. She knew he needed it as much as she did. She justified her feelings by reminding herself of how unhappy things were at home.

Everyone knew there were problems at home. Janet had been seen with a young graduate student. The rumors were beginning to swirl. The women could feel the tension. It was only a matter of time before someone made a mistake, and when it happened, Sophie wanted to be the one to console the good Reverend.

The phone rang. "Shady Grove Baptist Church, this is Sophie. Can I help you?"

"It's Deacon Andrews, Sophie. How you doing today?"

"It's been busy as usual, but God is good all the time." Sophie hated talking to the deacons. She knew they wanted to fire her on many occasions. She knew that Simon had gone to war to keep her job.

"I know that's right. Is the pastor in?"

"Yes he's in, but he's on the phone now. Do you want to leave a message?"

"Just tell him I called."

"I will."

"By the way, are you coming to the meeting Thursday?"

"I hadn't planned to, Deacon Andrews. Why?"

"I was hoping you could help us." His voice took on a different tone.

"I'll have everything you need for the meeting prepared ahead of time. The agenda and all copies will be ready. Do you need something else?"

"Well, you know the members are ready for a change." Andrews began his sales pitch.

"No, I didn't know that. Everyone I've talked to is quite happy." Sophie was ready to hang up.

"Not everybody is happy. People are fed up with Pastor. Things need to change and you can help us."

"I don't see how."

"You see things and you know things that nobody else knows. We need for you to tell us those things."

"I don't know what things you're talking about."

"Don't play stupid, Sophie. You know what I'm talking about. You know who he's sleepin' wit'."

"I don't know how I would know that. I wasn't there."

"Well, maybe you were there. You know people think he's screwin' you." Sophie smiled. At least the people have sense enough to see they made a good couple.

"I think I need to go now," Sophie snapped.

"There's no reason for you to get upset. We're willing to make it worth your effort. You help us and we'll help you."

"And who is us?"

"The deacons and trustees have met with some of the members and we took up a collection. If you give us something, we'll pay you for that information."

"You must be kidding! Never in my life have I heard such nonsense. You really think I would stoop that low! What kind of woman do you think I am?"

"The kind of woman who has been used. We know he's sleepin' with other women. You're not the only one, Sophie. Why should you come out lookin' like a fool to protect that so-called preacher? The least you could do is get something out of it."

Sophie wondered if it was true. Are there other women? What about Patsy? What about that woman on the phone? What about Bonita? She was willing to fight for Simon but not if she was being made into the fool.

"We collected $10,000. That's a lot of money. You know you need it, Sophie. All you have to do is tell the truth. You can keep your job. Nobody's blaming you. This man needs to be stopped. Too

many people have been hurt, and it's up to us to let the people know what's going on,"

There was a long silence.

•

Simon was surprised to hear from Jamaica. He had wondered where she was and if she ever thought about him. She entered his life and left it in one breath. She was his one-night stand. His affair. His fantasy.

He remembered the night as if it were yesterday.

It had been a long time since a woman intrigued him. The ups and downs of his marriage had drenched the flame. It seemed that nothing could rekindle the spark that caused him to propose. He wasn't sure if he'd ever loved. If so, it certainly wasn't the type of love that caused men to forget to eat. He got married because a baby was coming. It took all of his faith to keep him from straying. The task had been easy. That's until Jamaica walked in the room.

I have never seen a woman that beautiful before, was his first thought. He started with her head and made his way to her feet. Perfection. The curves were driving him wild. He wanted her badly. Each step was an act of seduction. Her jeans seemed to be painted on. As he examined the view from the rear she turned and smiled. She couldn't help but notice him sitting there with mouth wide open.

She walked toward him. The boldness could be felt as she kept her eyes glued on him. She glided across the room. He could hear music to match the well-choreographed stroll.

The frontal view was as alluring as the back. Her long hair was the perfect compliment to a face

that demanded respect. Her breasts stood attention, prepared for whatever came her way.

"My name is Jamaica." She wasted no time.

"I'm Simon." He was startled that she cared to meet him.

"I know who you are. Do you like what you see?" A mysterious smile curved her lips. She leaned forward to shake his hand, revealing the valley between her breasts.

"I'd be a fool not to." He took hold of her hand. His palm was warm and sweaty. The heat didn't stop there. He could feel the bulge between his legs. It was a feeling that had been missing for some time. He knew what time it was.

"How do you know me?" he smiled, hoping the answer would set the stage for the next step. He wasn't disappointed.

"Let's just say I've had my eyes on you for some time. I've been waiting for you to have your eyes on me." She grabbed a seat and got close enough to force him to whisper. "What's taken you so long?"

"I must be a fool. What can I do to make it up to you?" He could feel the flexing of his heart. He knew things were going too far but he lacked both the will and the way to remove himself from the game of words.

"No, it must have something to do with you being married. Everyone says you're too good to stray. I say you need to play." She flashed a sexy grin.

"That has been important to me. That and my faith in God." The mention of the marriage was the cold shower he needed.

"You don't have to play that with me. I know you better than you think." She read him like a

well-read novel. "Come with me. Let's go somewhere to talk." She reached out for his hand. It was an invitation to passion.

He felt a draw beyond the physical. There was something about this woman that intrigued him. He had to know how she knew him. Why she wanted him. There was a mystery that had to be solved. That was the reason he gave himself for taking her hand. The real reason was he wanted to play.

For the next three hours they talked. He discovered there was a brain behind the beauty. She was a graduate student majoring in journalism. She was a reporter for a local television station. Prior to becoming a reporter she was a model in New York. She decided that she wanted to be known for more than her looks and went back to school. Her long-range goal was to manage a television station.

She first saw Simon while covering a student protest. Simon spoke on behalf of the students who were demanding the hiring of black faculty and a freestanding black cultural center. "I wanted to scream when I heard you speak. I thought that you had the stuff to be another Martin or Malcolm. I saw our future as a people that day," Jamaica said.

After that day she had covered other functions where Simon participated. She listened to his prayers. She heard him speak. "I wanted to get to know you. I was prepared to introduce myself when I saw your wife hug you after a speech. I was hurt to discover you're married. I wished it were me. The more I watched the more I celebrated that it's not me."

"What do you mean?" They had become comfortable with one another. The conversation had moved from flirtation to intense friendship.

"I could tell that you're not happy. I felt sad for you."

"How could you tell?"

"It's the way you hug. It's the way you look at her. You can tell that you're only there because you think you have to be." She was right. He couldn't deny it. The only issue left to explore was how she fit into the puzzle.

They spent the night together. He woke up in her arms with no thoughts of how not going home would impact his marriage. He didn't care. He wanted the taste of Jamaica on his lips every day. He wanted to consider a life with a woman who made his heart beat faster.

Something had been lost along the way. She kissed him in places he never knew had sensation. They made love through the night. The heat of their lovemaking left them both drenched in sweat. He never forgot that night. He wanted more. He never got his chance.

Janet learned of the one-night stand and left Simon for another man. The word of the fling spread like wild fire throughout the city, forcing Simon to decide between what he felt and his career in ministry. Jamaica couldn't take the heat. She told Simon she wouldn't see him anymore. He struggled to get her out of his system. He wondered if it was the good sex or something deeper that pulled him in her direction. He never got a chance.

Now she was on the phone. After all these years of trying to find her, hoping to see her one last time, she calls.

"What's up big shot," she said. The voice was the same.

"I'm doing the best I can with what I've got," he laughed.

"So, you're finally in the big league, Mr. Big Time Pastor with the nosey secretary."

"I do my best girlfriend. What about you?"

"I'm living in Dallas now. I'm in your city for the next week," she said. "I read about you in the alumni magazine."

"You know I've been wondering about you."

"That's good to know. A sister likes to be thought of."

"I see you're still a flirt."

"Why stop? It's been working for me all these years." They both laughed. It was as if nothing had changed.

They talked about her work in Dallas with an ABC affiliate. She worked her way from a reporter to news anchor. She was considering a move to New York to work with the network. Simon wasn't surprised. She had the looks and the intelligence to go far in broadcast news.

"So, would you like to take a sister out to dinner?" She asked before he had a chance.

"You know you wrong," he chuckled. "You're supposed to let a brother ask you out."

"If I wait on a brother I might lose 10 pounds," she snapped back. "I been on the phone for 10 minutes and you haven't asked to see me yet. What's up with that?"

They decided to meet Tuesday night at the Washington Duke Hotel. They planned to meet after the funeral.

•

Sophie was still thinking about her conversation with Deacon Andrews. Over the years she had been faithful to Simon. She remained loyal because deep down she felt he wanted her. She had waited for him to acknowledge his desire, but he

never did. Ten thousand dollars is a lot of money. It was money that she could use.

Although she loved working with Simon, the job never paid her enough to satisfy all her needs. The benefits package failed to provide her with medical coverage or retirement. She was beginning to worry about what her life would look like after walking away from Shady Grove.

She looked at the phone. Simon was still talking to that woman. As she glanced at the phone again she heard laughter in his office. She could sense that this call was not about business. She felt her dream fading away in the mist of the conversation in the other room. How long would it take for Simon to embrace her? How long before she would be given a chance to prove to him that she was the woman to satisfy his thirst? She knew he wasn't happy at home. Why wouldn't he allow her to be the oasis he needed?

Sophie had rehearsed the conversation she prayed for. "I've been watching you. I know you need something. It's something I can give. No one else knows you like me. Let me be everything you need. I'll be your friend, your lover, and the partner you need." She never got her chance. Maybe she waited too long.

The laughter in the other room was getting louder. Who is this woman? What does she look like? Where did they meet? How long has she known him? Question after question clouded her mind.

Sophie had prayed for a man since her husband left her five years ago. She had what she thought was a happy union. No, it wasn't a perfect marriage, but they were building for themselves a life together that others admired. He left after they

purchased a new home. He left after being promoted to a new position. It happened suddenly. It took her by surprise.

She wasn't surprised that he was having an affair. She had heard the rumors of her husband stepping out on her to be with other women. It started after the birth of their second child. She gained a lot of weight, and this time she wasn't able to lose the extra pounds. Their sex life took a drastic turn for the worse after that. They would go weeks, sometimes months, without making love.

With the extra weight came a dive in her self-esteem. She would cry at night without understanding why. She assumed Ralph didn't want her anymore. Why would he? She was fat, with no college degree. He was attractive with two masters degrees. He made good money, and women threw themselves on him. She understood the game. She knew he was prone to stray, but never thought he would walk away from his family to be with another woman.

Sophie's response was the norm. She did what most black women do after catching their man with another woman. She called the bitch and told her to keep away from her man. She threatened to kick her ass. After that she slashed Ralph tires. All four. It didn't stop there. She did everything within her power to destroy his reputation. Her game backfired. Before long she found herself in a deep depression.

She came to Shady Grove in need of a change. She had lost all faith in men. What she discovered was how her actions helped contribute to the slide in her marriage. It was her preoccupation with the negatives that drove Ralph away. Why would a man want to stick around to listen to a woman complain all the time about how bad her life is? He

got tired of listening to her rant and rave about his lack of attention. She blamed him for her lack of accomplishments. It was his fault that she never graduated from college. It was his fault that she was overweight. It was because of him that she found herself miserable and confused.

Ralph walked away because he was tired of having a life filled with bad news. Sophie was the bad news. All she could see was a younger, smarter, prettier woman. She was the complete opposite of herself. In the end she learned that she hated herself and blamed Ralph for creating what she hated.

Simon helped her see all of that. He restored her faith in men. He taught her to love herself first and not to depend on anyone else to make her whole. She learned that her marriage was nothing but a series of lies. They stayed together because of children. Ralph may have never loved her, and if he did at one time, she couldn't blame him anymore for falling out of love. How could she when she found it difficult to love herself?

She was hired as the church administrative assistant after a series of conversations with Simon. He offered her the job after his previous assistant took a job out of state. He needed help fast, and she needed a job badly. That was a long time ago. She took the job hoping to gain more than a paycheck. She had fallen in love.

Over the years there were moments when she felt it coming. There was the day when she heard Simon crying. She went to his office to find him weeping with his face on his desk. She asked if she could help. He said nothing. She offered to hold him. He said no. She felt his need, but he kept his distance. Sophie understood why. He was a man of principle.

There were other times when he dropped a hint. "Pray for me Sophie. I'm having problems at home." She heard more than he said. She heard, "I'll be leaving Janet soon. Pray for me as I process out of my marriage." He never said all of that, but she knew that's what he meant.

There were the times when he asked her about her love life. She read his concern as a way to keep tabs on who she was dating. It was his way of making sure it wasn't too late. Simon would listen as she talked about her frustrations with dating. Men seemed okay until you let them get inside your house. Then the real motive is exposed. All they want is to get you in bed, and if they do, they will drop you once they get what they want, or they'll only call when they can't find someone else to give them what they want.

Sophie worked hard not to become a booty call. That wasn't easy. There were nights when she wanted to be a booty call. Like most women she had needs. She wanted to be held at night. She wanted to be told she's beautiful and desirable. She wanted to give herself to a man sexually, and there were times when she didn't care if she knew his name. Like anyone else, there were nights when she wanted to get her freak on.

Her friends would talk to her about their sexual escapades. Some of them had dated married men. They told her it was the best of both worlds. They would buy them nice things, pay their rent, take them out to nice places and go home to their wives. Once they went home they could call someone else and pretend none of it ever happened.

They would talk about how women needed to learn to think and act like men. When a man does it, he's a player. When a woman does it, she's a ho. This double standard had to be stopped, and the

only way to do that was for women to stop pretending that they feel differently than men about sex. Women want it just as much as men. There are times when a woman just wants a man to please her. He can go home after it's done. No strings attached. Her friends told her to take control of her sexuality. She heard them, but couldn't force herself to go there.

She was saving herself for Simon. Many days she sat at her desk envisioning Simon touching her between her legs. She imagined him kissing her gently on her lips, on that special place at the back of her neck, and licking her nipples. She could feel the heat there at her desk as she fantasized of his whispering in her ear, "I can't take it anymore. I have to have you now." The thought of his lifting her from her chair and placing her gently on his desk kept her going. There on his desk he would kiss her stomach. From there he'd slowly kiss his way to her warm garden.

Simon was off the phone. Ten thousand dollars is a lot of money.

Preacha' Man

Chapter Three – Tuesday

"The wages of sin is death"

"THAT WAS A FINE EULOGY, PASTOR," Mary Collins, one of the older members of the church said.

"Thank you, Sister Collins. Deacon Stanley meant so much to this church," Simon said as he held back his true feelings. He was glad it was over. He had spoken the last words over one of his strongest critics. He knew the worst fight was ahead of him. The death of Deacon Stanley was not the end of the vicious fight that was soon to come.

"You so right, Pastor," Collins continued. "He's been at this church longer than anybody. I'm sure gonna miss him."

Despite the hostility between Deacon Stanley and Simon, Simon would miss him too. He respected Stanley because of his willingness to stand, even if it meant they're standing on opposite ends of the battle. Simon didn't mind people having different opinions. His problem came when people assumed their opinion was the only one to consider.

Simon led the family and friends to the fellowship hall for dinner. They had just returned from the gravesite. The place was packed with people who came to support the family. Clergy came from across the district. Stanley was well known, respected and loved.

After Simon blessed the meal, a group gathered outside the church. These private meetings had become a common occurrence at Shady Grove. Deacon Andrews was in the middle of the group campaigning to oust the pastor during Thursday's special call meeting.

"He ain't preaching the word no more," Andrews said. "I ain't as concerned about some of the rumors as I am about his compromising the word of God. God has to be God folk. The word of God is true, and that man ain't preaching the unadulterated Gospel."

"That's been my problem too," chimed Chanti Stephens, a 35 year-old counselor. "It seems to me that he's been taking the word out of context to fit his own opinion. What we need is a person who will teach the word."

"Like that time when he told us we don't need to take communion," said Billie Ramond, the former superintendent of the Sunday School Department. "We work hard to teach our children certain principles and this man tears it all apart. Who does he think he is telling us that taking communion isn't important?"

"And what about this gay issue," Andrews said. "We told him he needed to take a stand against homosexuality and he told us he refused. We have a gay person in the pulpit and he won't say a word about it. He's compromising the word of God and God ain't pleased."

"I think you need to let the man alone," said Steve Cruz, a 38 year-old businessman who came to Shady Grove after spending time in prison. He came to Shady Grove because he heard Simon was a recovering addict who understood the needs of people with addictions. "The man helped save my life, and that's all that matters to me. I think you don't like him because he's different."

People started criticizing Simon after he locked his hair and began wearing an earring. Many of the members complained that he made the church look bad with his bad boy look. They wanted a more conservative pastor. They wanted him to go back to his old look, but he refused. One Sunday he stood before the people and told them he had a vision for a church that would reach the hip-hop crowd.

"Right is right, Steve," Andrews responded. "Shady Grove has become the laughing stock of the city. People laugh at us because they say everything goes over here. A line has to be drawn. People are leaving like crazy, and if we don't do something fast we're going to lose everything."

"Look at what the man has done," Steve snapped. "The church was small when he came. Look at how many people come here now. We built a new sanctuary. Look at all the young people who come. They come because of that man. Leave him alone instead of slamming him."

"God ain't pleased if we allow him to function in disobedience, Steve," Stephens added. "We are held responsible if we allow our leadership to rule outside the will of God and say nothing. We love him, but right is right and wrong is wrong. Did you hear what he said last week? He said sex before marriage is okay."

"I didn't hear him say that. I heard him say the problem with sex before marriage isn't just the joining of two bodies," Steve said. "I heard him say we have to consider the reason why it's wrong. It's because we abuse another person for our own gratification. You folks look for wrong and can't hear no right."

"All I know is our children are suffering," Billie Ramond said. "The kids need a role model, and he ain't the one."

"That's not what the kids say," Steve lashed back.

"What matters is what the people say," Andrews interrupted. "The people will be discussing this on Thursday night. I can't speak for no one else, but I'll tell you what. I'm tired of the mess. If he don't leave I'll leave."

"Good," Steve said. "That's what you need to do. You and all the other demons in this church. You all need to leave so God can do what God wants to do. This is stupid. The man has done no wrong. No, he ain't perfect, but he has helped bring us a long way."

There were many people in the church who supported Simon. The problem was the vast number of critics in leadership positions. Despite the massive growth within the ministry there had never been a time when people were satisfied with the work of the ministry. Many people condemned Simon for his inability to visit the sick and elderly on a consistent basis. They were right. Simon was lacking in this area. He was deficient because of the need to pick up the pace in other key areas. He had come to depend on the deacons to do the visitation, yet the members had an expectation that he was not always able to fulfill.

The membership had grown from 300 to over 2,000 since he arrived. The massive growth was, in part, the result of his community involvement. Shady Grove was known as a church with a pastor who had a heart for the community. Many of the members didn't share his vision for the community. They saw the growth, but refused to acknowledge it as the work of God. They couldn't because it went against what they believed the church should be.

Simon was a shining star in the community. He seemed to have everything going his way. The truth is his confidence was beginning to falter and his pastoral competence waned under the attacks. They began to accuse him of substance abuse, extramarital affairs, homosexuality, and mental disorders.

He was under severe attack. People didn't just disagree or criticize, they insisted on inflicting pain and damaging Simon. The attacks never stopped. There were times when they went underground, where tactics changed, but the critics were willing to break any rules of decency to accomplish their destruction.

Deacon Andrews and his gang were deceitful. They would manipulate, camouflage, misrepresent, and accuse others of their own attacks. They were evil. Simon became the symbol and scapegoat for the internal pain and confusion they felt. Andrews presented himself as a pious, active church member who was only doing this for the good of the church. He had convinced numerous naïve parishioners that he was raising legitimate issues.

Andrews found power in fighting openly. He intimidated Simon by letting everyone know that he was willing to fight dirty and use any tactic to gain

his ends. Many of the members stayed on the sidelines, allowing Simon and Andrews to cope the best they could. Andrews knew how to throw a tantrum to get his way. He knew how to distract, confuse and seduce. He had wounded by direct attack. He had used others to inflict wounds.

Simon was bleeding and trying to survive, and had little energy available to be creative in ministry. He did his best to continue to provide services for the masses, and because of his visibility, many did not realize that he was deeply injured. Hardly anyone came to him with the kind of understanding, strength and support he needed. He took personally the negative climate in the church. When people talked about being unhappy, he perceived it as his fault. His reaction was to try harder to fix what had gone bad. The problem was that most of the causes of decline had deep, historical roots, and because of that past, he wasn't able to reverse the trend alone. In trying to fix things on his own, Simon was neglecting his own physical, mental and spiritual discipline. This made him even more vulnerable.

Simon returned to his office to unwind after the dinner. The thing on his mind was the conversation he had with Patsy the day before and the date he had later with Jamaica. Patsy was one of the few people who understood what he needed. The problem was with what he needed. He felt a tremendous burden in his spirit. How could he justify needing a relationship with a woman given his role as the pastor of the church?

He needed the embrace of a woman. Someone who could take the pain away. He knew that Thursday's meeting could mark the end of his tenure at Shady Grove. Simon was angry about that possibility, yet thrilled over the chance to enter into

another life. Ministry had taken a big dent out of his soul. No longer did he bring the passion he once did. No longer did he believe in the truths that led him to accept his call into ministry. He loved God, but had come to hate the church. The rules and structure of the church were interfering with the real work of kingdom building. He wasn't certain if he could continue to function in a church that refused to move beyond its historical understanding of what it means to be God's people.

An example was the church's old position on homosexuality. Simon was seeking a place where people could be loved and supported beyond their lifestyle choices. Why couldn't the church love gay people? Why was it important that they bash gays? Why was he being labeled as one who compromised the gospel because of his unwillingness to cast all gays to Hell?

There was a time when Simon could do that. That time had passed him by. He was now seeking harmony in the church. He wanted a place where people could discover a way to discuss their differences without judgment. Why couldn't people of faith talk about homosexuality? Why is it so controversial to push for an open dialogue on the subject? Simon no longer understood the position of the church, and was beginning to wonder if he was the problem. Maybe it was time for him to step back.

The only thing that kept him at Shady Grove was the people who supported him. That and his fear over what would come of his life if he walked away. So many people encouraged him not to give up. They, like him, wanted to move past the God talk to the God walk. So many times he had challenged the congregation not to be so in love with

the things they believe, that they're not able to do the things God calls them to do. He wanted to make a difference in the community. The city needed that. Too many were still hooked on drugs. Crime was out of control, yet despite it all, the issue for the people was his termination.

Was it necessary for him to do God's work from a pulpit? Should he allow a few angry people to push him away from the work that God called him to do? Was he the problem or was he functioning in a way modeled after the work of Christ?

Maybe he had become too radical. The locks and earring were an instant shock among the people. Simon had to stop to ask himself if he was going through a midlife crisis, or if he had made a decision to change his appearance for the right reason. His final analysis was a combination of the two. His change of appearance was in response to his need to stand against the status quo. He no longer wanted to be perceived as normal. He did it because he was fed up with church that refused to honor the culture of the radicals in the midst. Those who desired an afrocentric look that is spiritually based needed to be heard and understood.

He couldn't change what he had done. He didn't want to. It was liberating to step outside the short cut fade, and black suit and white shirt look. Simon felt more at peace with his new look. The problem is the negative stuff that came with the decision. The new look combined with his radical theology became the talk of the town, and the fuel that led many to call for his head on a silver platter.

What would he do if they decided to fire him? His education prepared him for what he was doing, but he wasn't certain how it would translate to the world outside the church. He had a Master of

Divinity and Doctorate from Princeton Theological Seminary. Was that enough? Could he work a 9 to 5 job after all these years? Would he be paid what he had become accustomed to making? Did any of that matter?

What he needed was a safe place to hide. A place to run and scream. He needed someone to help him forget how screwed up his life had become. He was tired of the stares and glares coming from the people. Everywhere he went he could feel the criticisms. He knew the people were talking, and he knew most of what was being said was rumor. He couldn't bear responsibility for the things people made up. The thing that bothered him were the things they said that he wanted to do.

There were many nights when he thought of getting high again. It was the logical escape from the calamity. All he needed was one hit. A joint, a bottle, a whiff of cocaine—anything to take him away from the mass confusion. He almost relapsed five years earlier. It was after a church business meeting.

Eighteen years down the drain, he thought after leaving the church. After 18 years of doing the right thing, he was ready to give up. The pain of the attack was more than he could bear. Sunday after Sunday he preached concerning the presence of God. Week after week Simon preached comfort to the weary souls who approached the throne of God's grace. Week after week, Sunday after Sunday he pronounced deliverance to oppressed servants. He proclaimed good news to the least of these. After the attack, Simon searched deep within for that good news.

"Rev., you gonna be all right?" one of the faithful sisters of the church asked as Simon prepared to leave the church.

"I'll be okay. God is able. The Lord has a way of working things out," the Preacha' Man spoke. Did He really believe that? Simon had become so accustomed to saying the right thing. The words flowed from his lips like cruise control. "The Lord will provide. Just wait on the Lord. Wait I say. Wait I say. The Lord will come. May not come when you want, but he's right on time. The Lord will never put more on you than you can bear."

Words. Words of comfort. Words to support the weary. Words so easily spoken. Did he believe them? Could he trust them? Simon wanted to believe them. He wanted to cling to them. Words, breathe. Words, protect. Words, rescue. Words, comfort. Words, words, words.

"If you need anything, Rev., give me a call," the faithful sister promised. The sincerity of her voice helped soothe the rage. Simon knew that there were many like her in the church. Many who stood for him and with him. Many who understood his pain. Many who read through the veil of strength. Many who desired to be his friend. Many who wanted to talk.

Could Simon trust them? He trusted the Judas who led the attack. Many Judases had risen over the years. Many turned their back on Simon. The man in Simon wanted to trust. The preacha' man, the strong fake side, refused to give in. "Be strong," the voice of the preacha' man demanded. "Don't give in! She's like the others."

"Just pray with me, Sister. We have to understand that what happened tonight was the work of the devil. We can't allow ourselves to hate

those who attack us, but rather we must understand that they are used by the devil to do the work of evil. Like Peter who told Jesus he could not die. We are challenged to love them despite what they do to us," the words.

Eighteen years down the drain. Is it worth the pain? Simon walked to his beat up Olds '98. The car was on its last leg. One hundred and sixty-seven thousand miles and barely moving. He had spent hundreds of dollars over a three-month period to keep it running. He opened the back door and threw his briefcase on the back seat. In his briefcase was the work for the evening. His Bible for study, Samuel Proctor's book, *The Substance of Things Hoped For*, and the outline for Sunday's sermon. The work had to continue. Despite the attack, Simon had to go on. He had to prepare for Sunday—for the words—despite the rebuke.

One hundred and sixty-seven thousand miles and no money to buy another car. His budget would not allow for another expense. Two thousand dollars a month after taxes. Student loans, bills on top of bills, and four in the household. No other source of income. At the time, Janet couldn't find a job after being let go. One hundred and sixty-seven thousand miles with $2,000 a month. How will he pay for the children's education? How will he... Too many questions. No answers.

"How could they refuse to give me a raise?" The pain of the question made Simon shake. "How could they, how could they, how could they not give me a raise? How could they not see what we have accomplished? How could they not see what I have helped to create? How could they not care about the needs of my family?"

One hundred and sixty-seven thousand miles and no money. Simon turned the ignition. It started. As he pulled out of the parking lot, he noticed that the meeting after the meeting had started. Groups had gathered outside the church. One in the parking lot behind the church. One in front of the church. Another in front of the church annex. He wondered what they were saying. He knew that it was about him. He knew that they would use this occasion to drag his name in the mud.

Eighteen years down the drain. Eighteen years of ministry. Eighteen years of marriage. Eighteen years of being strong. Eighteen years of pretending—pretending to be strong, pretending to be holy, pretending to be satisfied. Eighteen years of sacrifice. Eighteen years of trusting, believing, hoping, praying, fasting, waiting, enduring, and giving. Eighteen years of catching hell from black folks. Eighteen years of being talked about, falsely accused. Eighteen years of doing the best he could to overcome temptations.

"I can't take this crap anymore." Voices from the past swirled through his mind. Voices from the past begging to re-emerge. Voices begging Simon to re-visit old playgrounds, old play things. Eighteen years after his last drag from a joint. Eighteen years after his last snort of cocaine. Eighteen years after preaching about and living the life of recovery—Simon thought of getting high.

"What difference does it make?" voices from the past challenged. "Who will know? You need an escape. No one loves you. No one cares. You can't stand the pressure alone," voices begged for a hit.

The tears were heavy now. Simon couldn't stop them. Gallons of tears soaked his face and dripped like heavy rain on his chest. Too many

questions without answers. Too many demands made without resources to fulfill them. Too much to do, too little time to sustain it all. Voices and tears, voices and tears. Why, cry; what, cry; how, cry. Back and forth between tears and questions Simon maneuvered as he drove to the place his clients talked about. He drove looking for drugs.

Eighteen years down the drain. In that moment Simon forgot how to pray. He forgot how to wait. He needed a friend to heal the pain. He forgot that Jesus is a friend in times of need. He forgot the rock in the weary land, the leaning post. He forgot the words of the church, and sought the comfort of the streets. He drove and cried. He drove and pleaded. Simon drove himself to buy some crack.

Simon wanted a new escape. The church had turned it's back on him, and he needed a place to heal. The house of healing—the church—had turned on him. He had come to the church for help 18 years earlier. He came needing help and the church, the people in it, opened their arms and provided him what he needed—unconditional love. Through their loving him Simon found himself. By receiving their love he gained what he was missing the most—a family who cared enough to meet him where he was. He was dead. They came into his grave and pulled him out. They cried over his dead bones until new life entered the weary bones of his despair.

Eighteen years later the church was found failing. He continued to need its love and support. Simon continued to need its unconditional acceptance. Instead he found the rebuke of a mad mob of lynch men. Crucify, crucify! What happened to the community of love that had helped

elevate him to higher heights? What happened to the voice of reason in the crowd? The voice that calls for unity and peace? Where was the power of God's spirit that allows people like Simon to move beyond the pain? Eighteen years down the drain.

He turned left onto Angier. He drove down Angier looking for a hit. They were everywhere. Less than a half-mile from the church the dealers were camped out waiting for despairing fools—like Simon. Young hoods with pockets full of money and guns hooked to their sides filled the streets. Young dealers were strategically placed on each side of the street. On the left side one of the young dealers counted his stash of cash. On the other side a dealer stared Simon down as he approached his space. Simon could read his mind, "What this nigger want?" Hookers yelled, "Hey," as he passed by. One licked her lips. Another rubbed her thighs.

Simon slowed down. He was ready to bust a move. He stopped his beat up Olds '98 in the middle of the heat. Eleven fifteen on a Thursday night. Hookers everywhere. The smell of crack in the air. Violence waiting to crawl in the back seat. Death waiting to take Simon home.

"Yo, what ya need?" His impatient glare caught Simon by surprise. His look said don't waste my time.

"What you got?" it was all Simon knew to say.

"Depends on what ya want and what ya got."

"You got some crack?" The words slipped between Simon's lips like a ruined CD. "You got some crack?" He said that? Did he ask him for that? What are you thinking? Again, thoughts circled Simon's mind.

"You the police, bro?" he demanded. His street savvy was clear. It reminded Simon of the

time when he was approached by a narc. Simon was walking from the hospital and he pulled up beside him. He asked, "Want a ride?" It was cold and Simon was tired. He took him up on his offer. Once inside his car he asked where he could buy some weed. He said he was new in town and was looking to set up an operation. He could read through his line of bull. Why did he stop Simon? He knew Simon's routine. He was waiting for him to get off from work. Simon was too slick for that.

This young hood had smarts. Simon looked in his eyes. He could be a successful businessman. He had street smarts and that could take him far. As Simon looked at him he forgot the question.

"Yo man, you the police?" He was getting impatient with Simon. There was business to be had, and he wanted his share of the action.

"No," Simon answered. Pain filled his soul. No, I'm not the police, I'm the preacha' man from down the street. I pastor that big church over on East End. I'm the one who's always fussing about the crime in the streets. I'm the one who's putting pressure on the police to lock people like you up. I'm the one who helped organize the Partners Against Crime project in this area. I'm the one who works with addicts and young hoods like you. That's what Simon was thinking. I'm not the police—I'm the preacha' man.

Guilt and shame settled in. Simon took another look at the young entrepreneur standing beside his car. He looked hard. He was looking for something to sustain him. Something to protect him.

"Ya got twenty, bro?" He was ready to close the deal. "Yo, what ya need?" The words would not let Simon rest. How did he end up here?

Simon looked and saw what he was afraid of. As he looked at the businessman outside his car, he saw himself. Eighteen years down the drain. This is what he used to be. This is what he once lived for. Hiding from the police and making money off of other people's pain. He once lived for moments like this. Simon looked at the brother outside the car and saw himself 18 years earlier. This is what he used to be. This is what God changed in him.

"That's all right, man." Simon pulled away from the heat. As Simon drove away the dealer yelled at him. The prostitutes tried to wave him down. The young dealers looked at Simon like he was a mad man looking for trouble. He rolled up his window and locked the door and drove home to prepare his Sunday sermon.

That was then. Since that night Simon became more vocal about his addiction. Hiding from his struggle became part of the struggle. One way to fight the urge was to share his story with the people. Many people didn't understand. They perceived it as his way of glamorizing his life. Others used it against him by claiming that he still had a drug problem.

"You need anything before I leave, Pastor," Sophie asked as she walked past Simon's office.

"No, I should be okay. We have everything ready for Thursday's meeting?"

"The agendas are ready and the copies will be made tomorrow."

"Good."

"I have something to ask you if you don't mind," Sophie asked. It was time to make her move.

"No problem. Come on in." Sophie stepped into Simon's office and closed the door.

"I don't want anyone to hear our conversation. You don't mind if I close the door, do you?"

"No, that's fine."

Sophie was tense. She wondered if it was the wrong time to bring up the subject. With everything that was happening around the church Simon was stressed to the point of no return. She understood better than anyone the massive demands on his life. He needed a break, and he didn't need additional drama.

"What I have to ask you is about me," Sophie started.

"Is everything okay at home?"

"No, that's not it. It's about my work here."

"Now, don't be quitting on me."

"With everything that's going on around here the thought has crossed my mind. The only thing that has kept me here is you, Pastor. If it weren't for you and your support I don't think I could have made it this far. These folks around here are crazy. I don't know how you do it."

"It's not as bad as it appears." Both of them knew that was a lie.

"Well, I'm not leaving unless you leave. I can't leave, Pastor, because of how I feel about you. I've stayed because I feel God placed me here to be a support for you. I've done my best to be that support. Now I want to do more for you. I want to help you in any way I can. Do you understand?" This was the moment she had been waiting for.

"You want more responsibility. I can arrange that. You have grown and we should honor that by giving you more of a creative role."

"That's not what I mean, Pastor. What I'm saying is I want to be there for you, not the church. I want to give myself to you."

Her cards were on the table. "I believe God brought me here to be the woman you need."

Simon didn't know what to say. He feared hurting Sophie's feelings, but needed to establish a firm boundary.

"Sophie, you know I think the world of you. You have helped me tremendously since you came on board. I care deeply for you, but I can't give myself to you the way you want. I hope you understand. There has to be a line drawn. I am the pastor. As the pastor, I can't have a relationship with any women in the church. That's not to mention the fact that I am married. I am a man of God. I'm flattered, but I can't be what you want me to be."

The truth hurt. "So, you have led me on? Is that what you're saying to me?"

"What do you mean I led you on?"

"You gave me every reason to believe that you felt for me the same as I felt for you. You come into my office and flirt with me. You buy me nice gifts and tell me how special I am, and now you're saying you didn't mean any of that."

"No, I did mean all of that. I meant it as a boss to an employee. I meant it as a friend who understood the line that has to be drawn. I have never allowed myself to think of having a relationship with you because it's out of order. I couldn't think about it, and you shouldn't have been thinking of it."

"That's a lie, Simon. I've seen you look at my legs. I've watched you look at me like you wanted me."

"That may be true, but that doesn't mean I was willing to take it to the next level. I can't do that."

"So, it's okay for you to screw everyone else. It's okay for you to have relationships with other women in and outside of the church, but you can't with me. You're a hypocrite, Simon."

"What are you talking about?"

"I know who you're with. I keep your schedule. I see them come in your office. What about you and Bonita? What about Patsy? How about that woman on the phone with you yesterday? You can pretend that you're so holy, but I know the real deal."

"That's not true, Sophie. Not everything is what it looks like."

"Do you think I'm a fool? You knew I was interested in you. You led me on and used me. I've given myself to you, protected you, supported you, and closed my ears to all the rumors, even when it seemed they might be true. I did that all for you, and what do you do in return? You used me. You led me on to believe we had something special."

"How did I do that? By being nice to you?"

"No, you did it by creating an atmosphere where I thought it could be. Answer this for me, Simon. Have you ever wanted me?"

"No, I haven't."

"You're telling me the thought never crossed your mind."

"I'm sorry, the thought never crossed my mind."

"So you were playing me," Sophie cried. "You played me for a fool. I gave myself to you all these years for nothing."

Sophie stormed out of the office and slammed the door. Simon was shocked by her reaction. As he processed their time together he sought to determine if Sophie was justified in being angry. He had to be honest about one thing, there were many times when he looked at her legs and wondered what it would be like to make love to her. The weak, hurting part of himself wanted to use her to satisfy his own need, but he knew it was the last thing she needed. What she needed was a man who was willing and able to commit for the long haul. He couldn't do that. He couldn't see himself with her beyond a few rolls in the hay.

How do you tell a woman you've fantasized about making love without setting her up to be hurt? Knowing how she felt about him made it harder for him to draw the line. It would have been easy to use her up, and move on after all the dust was settled. Why not, that's what people rumored him to be. Why not become what they claimed?

Simon spent more time pushing women away than he did in pursuing them. It would have been easy for him to make love to Bonita. The problem was Bonita wanted more than he could give. They came close. He walked away after she told him the next dick to enter her vagina would be the last. He knew he would not be the last. He had to walk away.

Patsy was his dream woman. Many days had passed with the thought of being with her on his mind. The thing that stopped him was her connection to the church. He couldn't take advantage of the members. He knew that Patsy would be more than a one-night stand. He wanted her for more than a ride. He wanted all of her, and the thought of not being able to have her because of his marriage scared him. He knew that he would

walk away from his marriage and work to be with her, and he wasn't ready to make that sacrifice.

He wanted to be different than the other men he knew in ministry. So many of his friends in ministry justified their extramarital affairs. They pointed to the lives of the giants of the faith—Martin Luther King, Jr. and others. It's part of the male struggle. It doesn't offset the work of God. God understands our burden. That's what they said.

Although he was having problems at home he didn't want to get caught up in using women to place band-aids on his pain. It was better that he deal with the reality of his situation than bring an innocent person into the equation. He fought the impulse. He loved making love, and he, like many of his friends in ministry, liked variety. He enjoyed the wild things in life. He wanted a woman who could take him to places he'd never been before. He wanted to be reminded of how good a man he was, instead of hearing the constant nagging about what he needed to do.

Simon had not been a perfect husband. He had an affair. He remembered how hurt he was when it happened. It didn't solve anything, in fact, it made matters worse. An affair with Sophie would be a disaster. Her problem with perception could get him in trouble. Before long, the entire church would know about the affair and he would be out the door. He couldn't give them anything to use against him. The rumors were bad enough. The truth could take him down.

•

"Janet, are you sure you want to do this?" The school counselor knew her by first name. She had spent enough time at the school to be on payroll. Janet and Simon believed in parental involvement. No one would be caught taking

advantage of their kids. The staff at the school respected them for caring enough to be involved.

"Yeah, Deloris, I'm sure," Janet answered. "I've already accepted the job at the University of Chicago. There's no reason for me to stay. It's time to move on."

"I'm sorry to hear that. I know you've had problems, but this is taking me by surprise." Deloris and Janet had become friends over the years. Janet came to her for counseling when things had gotten out of control.

"It's not just Simon. I can't deal with the first lady thing anymore. The people stay in your business so much that you can't take a shit without someone making a movie. I'm tired of that life. I need to move on to something different."

"How is Simon taking all of this"?

"I haven't told him yet. I was waiting for things to calm down before I told him, but it doesn't look like things will ever calm down. You've heard about the meeting on Thursday?"

"Yeah girl, it's the talk of the town."

"I still love Simon, but things have changed so much over the years. I miss the old Simon. He's lost his passion and our marriage died a long time ago. If he's not having an affair, it won't be long before he does. The sad thing is I wouldn't blame him if he did."

"I know you're lying about that."

"He's got to get the booty from somewhere, and he ain't getting it from me."

"What's that about?"

"It's about both of us being so tired and angry over shit that's so damn old that neither one of us can remember the script. The same ole, same ole has been going on for so long that we can't remember what it was like when there wasn't any drama."

"That's sad, girlfriend."

"Not as sad as what's happening to me."

"What do you mean?"

"Let's just say that if Simon had an affair I couldn't be angry because of my stuff."

"What!"

"What was I supposed to do? A girl's got needs, too. I was tired and frustrated. I needed a man to remind me of how special I am. I wasn't looking for it, but it sure found me."

"Where did you find him?"

"Don't laugh. You promise not to laugh?"

"I ain't promising nothing, but girl you know my shit stinks so tell me anyway."

"I met him at a bachelorette party."

"What?"

"He was the stripper."

"You go girl! I know he's fine."

"You got that right! And the brother can move a mountain and calm the raging sea."

"Tell me more."

"After the show, he pulled me aside and asked if we could get together. I told him I was married. He said, "I didn't ask you that." He caught me during a weak time. You know just before the red sea hit. The next thing I knew I was at his place doing the doggy." Janet laughed at herself.

"So, it was just a one time thang."

"No, that's the bad part. Although he's a stripper, there's more to him than that. We talked. We have so much in common. He likes old movies. He loves jazz, just like me. We enjoyed each other and kept in contact after that night."

"Don't tell me it's serious, girl."

"Not as serious as I'd like. There's a big snag."

"What's that?"

"The Sunday after we hooked up, I go to church. I'm sitting in my normal seat and guess who walks in?"

"No!"

"The stripper walks in the place with some girl. He's a member of the church. He loves Simon like a brother."

"Oh, my God!"

"We decided we cared too much about each other to let it die. We've kept in on the down low, but it's killing both of us. How do you tell your husband you're fucking one of the members, and that he's a stripper on the side?"

"What does mister stripper think about your move?"

"He may be coming with me."

"What? Girl you must have whip appeal."

"Like I said, we enjoy each other. He's more than a stripper. He's a grad student who strips to pay for his education. The brother's finishing his MBA, and is considering a few jobs in Chicago."

"That's deep."

"The problem is with the kids. I don't want to expose them to too much too soon. He has a little girl. We're taking it one day at a time."

"Have you told the children?"

"No, I'll tell them tomorrow after I tell Simon."

"You're going to tell him before the meeting?"

"What else can I do?"

"I hope the deacons don't find out about this before that meeting."

"I can't control that, Deloris. I have to take care of me. If you ask me, Simon needs to get out

anyway. They don't appreciate him. They treat him like a dog after all he has given to that church."

"Sounds like a woman standing by her man."

"Despite all that has happened, Simon is my friend. I do love him; I'm just not in love with him. I want what's best for him, and I don't think Shady Grove is the best for him. "

"Why won't he leave?"

"I don't know. He talks about needing to have some stability with the family. You know he still feels guilty about moving us all over the damn country as he worked his way up the ladder. He's turned down so many opportunities to move. I don't know what it is about Shady Grove."

"Maybe he just loves the people."

"That's for sure, but they don't love him as much as he loves them. If they knew how deeply he cared they wouldn't take him through this."

"They say they love him."

"I know. Their 'I love you' is always followed by 'but'. 'I love you, but'. I have a problem with that."

"I know Janet. I remember the church before you came."

"It was a little church with a few crazy niggers. Look at them today. It's like they're saying, thank you for bringing us this far, now hurry along so we can find someone to carry on."

'It's so crazy."

"Yeah, it is. I wish I could be there for Simon, but I have to move on with my life. He needs to move on too."

•

"I'll have the Baja California Chicken and she'll have the Mahi Mahi." Simon ordered for Jamaica. She once told him she liked a man who

listened and took charge. She told him what she wanted.

"You know I like that," Jamaica chuckled. "You must be prepared to steal my heart."

"I was hoping I'd already done that. You mean I have some work to do?"

"It never hurts to keep working, my brother. Never take a woman for granted."

"You know that goes both ways, my sister. Don't take a good brother for granted." They both laughed. The waiter enjoyed himself. Simon looked around to see who was in the room.

"What's wrong, Simon," Jamaica asked. "Scared you might be seen."

"You know how it is being in the limelight."

"Well, don't worry. Black folks don't hang out here. I checked it out before I called you."

"That sounds like premeditation to me."

"No, it's more like a sister knowing a brother. Remember, I've been down that road before." The conversation was beginning to take on a serious note.

"How can I forget?" Simon reached out to touch her hand. "It's been on my mind since you walked away from me." Jamaica was more dazzling than Simon remembered. That was saying a lot. Age and money had served her well. Every man in the restaurant had taken notice of her. Her red dress hugged all the right places. The dress was the perfect compliment to her caramel toned skin. Her hair was braided to her waist.

"It's been on my mind too, Simon. I've often wondered what life would have been like if we had met at another time."

"Why did you walk away? Why didn't you ever call?"

"I couldn't deal with your situation. Your being married was one thing. Your line of work is another. I couldn't take the chance of having my reputation tarnished by being involved with a minister. That doesn't look good for a person in my line of work."

"I know. We've had that talk."

The jazz band was playing 'Round Midnight. Both Simon and Jamaica loved jazz. It was one of the things that brought them together.

"So, how's married life, Simon?"

"Worse than ever. I think we're headed to a divorce."

"I've heard that before. What's the hold up if things are so bad? Why haven't you done it before now?"

"I'm scared of what the people will say. You know it doesn't look good when a minister is divorced. Right now is a tough time for me. I'm not sure what will happen next." Simon felt himself ready to break. He needed to talk.

"What's that all about?"

"Let's just say things aren't great in ministry. I've changed. The people aren't happy. Some want me out, and they get their chance on Thursday."

"Yeah, I noticed your new look. I like it. It says something about you and the way you see ministry. I really like it."

"Thanks. The problem is some people don't see it the same way. They want to keep me in a box, and I'm breaking out of the box. I'm fed up with the old school interpretation of what it means to be a Christian. I'm ready to reach a new generation. I want to get as radical as I can. That's what got me in trouble."

"That sounds like a big step. So, how's the wife taking all of this?"

"We don't talk much about it. She's been busy with her work at the university. She comes home late at night. I can't tell you the last time we've talked about anything meaningful."

"Sounds to me like things are the same."

"No, things are worse. Much worse. I never thought I would say that. I was ready to leave before. Now it feels like it's already over. The only thing missing is the paper work. The question is who will step first."

Jamaica gave him that look. It was the look he'd missed. "I want you to kiss me right now, and don't say no," she whispered.

He kissed her gently. "No," she snapped. "I want you to kiss me like you've missed me. Like you've wanted me and needed me. I've waited all these years for your kiss. Kiss me like you mean it."

There in the middle of the room, in the presence of a crowd, Simon kissed Jamaica. The kiss helped him forget what he feared. Like old times it reminded him of what mattered. Love matters. He didn't want to stop. She didn't want him to stop.

"This night is about me and you," she whispered as she held his hand and peered into his eyes. "Tonight we both forget what we screwed up. We forget what we fear. All I want is to remember the best day of my life. That was the day I met you Simon. I want to remember loving like that."

"All these years I thought it was just me. I've believed you walked away because I wasn't good enough for you."

"You silly little boy," she chuckled. "I walked away because you were what I needed. I couldn't stand simply to play with you. I wanted all of you, and since I couldn't have it all I decided to

not pretend. I never thought that would happen when we first met."

"What did you think would happen?"

"I thought we'd have good sex and go home."

"Did I ever tell you that you talk and act like a man?"

"No, but that's why you love me so much." They both laughed. "You need a sister who's as freaky as you."

"You got that right."

"I'm not ashamed to tell you what I want. I called you because we had good sex. I want you to take me upstairs and fuck my brains out. After we finish I want to hold you like we did the first time. I'll tell you I love you and need you. I might cry. After we're done we'll go our separate ways. I'll wish I had you every day."

Neither finished their dinner. They embraced as soon as the door closed. Within seconds they both were coming out of their clothes. Their lips never parted as linen fell to the floor, piece by piece. Once completely naked they held one another. They took turns kissing each other's necks.

He loved the feel of her breasts. The years hadn't tainted their firmness. He kissed them the same way he did when they last met. The response was the same. She moaned. As he licked her left breast, he took his thumb and index finger and played with the right nipple.

She found his penis. It was already hard, as if to say, 'Take me.' The veins popped from its base to the beginning of the hat. She remembered how to stroke it. His moan matched hers.

He paused from his play with her breast to gaze into her eyes. A teardrop fell from the right

eye. He kissed it. "I will always love you," he whispered. "I will always need you."

"I will always love you," she answered. "No matter what happens."

He kissed her stomach. Her moan intensified with each taste. He went lower with each breath until he found her warm spot. He opened her legs and licked her clitoris. He sucked it the way she told him she liked it. He was driving her wild. He then placed his finger inside her as he sucked. "That's the way I like it, baby," she whispered in his ear.

As her insides became moist, she took his penis and placed it in her mouth. She licked the tip, then the sides. She teased him long enough to drive him wild, and then placed all of his hard penis in her mouth. "It's yours baby," Simon cried. "Take all of it. Take all of it."

"It's yours too, baby. That's your pussy."

Together they pleased one another. Together they climaxed—in each other's arms, one on top of the other. Each licking and sucking the other until there was nothing left to give. It was the beginning of a long night of lovemaking. With each passing hour they found the strength to make love over and over again. They made love like it might be the last time. As far as they knew it might be the last time. Neither was willing to waste a second. They had no time to waste. They had too much to say with their bodies, and each wanted to say it all.

The sun rose with them holding each other. The time passed too soon. As promised, Jamaica cried in Simon's arms. Simon returned the favor by crying in her arms. It was too good to be true. It felt so right, but they both knew it was all so wrong. How could something so good be wrong?

After so many years of being apart, the two reunited to discover true love never dies. Even when it is complicated by circumstances that make it impossible to take things to the next level, true love doesn't fade. Their love was real. The bad news was the passage of time had not changed the circumstances surrounding their lives. Simon was still married and involved in ministry, and Jamaica was still a journalist.

Preacha' Man

Chapter Four – Wednesday

"The truth will set you free"

GOING HOME WAS THE HARDEST PART. It was especially difficult given the recollections of what happened the last time Simon and Jamaica got together. The guilt and shame that follows an act of infidelity began to settle in. Maybe the people are right. Maybe Simon needed to be ousted as pastor. It was on his mind, and he couldn't make it go away. For all these years he had struggled to live his life in a way that represented God and his profession well. He didn't want to become another hypocritical black preacher. Did last night prove that he was no different?

There was one big difference. He loved Jamaica. She wasn't used to cover some deep pain. Being with her was more than just a one-night stand. He wanted her badly. The more he thought about last night and the years since they were last together, the more he came to understand that Jamaica was the only woman he had ever loved.

Why was the timing always bad? Why did his work have to hinder his ability to be with the woman of his dreams? No one was able to make him feel like Jamaica. She knew all the right buttons to press, and she knew when to press them. Other women wanted him for all the wrong reasons. With Jamaica, he knew that she loved him for all the right reasons. She knew him, yet still cared.

Many women became fascinated with men in the pulpit. There's something about the glamour of being in front of masses of people sharing words intended to inspire. Women seemed to be turned on to the power that came with the man in the pulpit. He has, so they think, a direct connection to God. Many feel he's next to God. Simon knew that many of the women who had expressed an interest in him were turned on more by what he did than by who he was. That wasn't true with Jamaica.

Women also liked the security that came with the minister. His salary had become the subject of conversation in the community. Pastor's salaries are open to public knowledge, and people like to brag about what their pastor gets paid, or complain about them being paid too much. Since Simon's compensation eclipsed $100,000, people began to point fingers at him. All women knew was that's a lot of money, and not many brothers can say the same. If you're going to seduce a man, why not go after one who has money, power and fame.

The thing that these women didn't know was what it took to get to that point. They were amused by an image, but knew nothing about the man behind the facade. They didn't know how he struggled to get to where he was. They didn't know that he sacrificed by taking low pay as the church grew to its current membership and budget. They didn't know how his family suffered to get to this

place, and how he was still burdened financially by decisions made long ago. All they knew was what they saw today. They didn't know the man. They loved the image.

Jamaica didn't care about any of that. Simon unlocked the door expecting to catch hell as soon as he walked in. It was 6:30 a.m. He had no real excuse for being out so late. He decided not to lie. What difference would it make? She wouldn't believe him anyway. For the past few months she had been on him about her assumption that he was having an affair with Bonita. He was certain that her name would be raised. He couldn't blame her.

Hurting Janet hurt Simon more than anything. It hurt him more than the issues with the church. As his hand reached for the doorknob he made an admission. Janet has been a good wife. She has been a wonderful mother. She has been his best friend. She has done everything she could to stand by his side. She has forgiven him and loved him when he did her wrong. She is worthy of love. She deserves respect. Why had he treated her this way?

The emotions began to come. He did his best not to cry, but he couldn't help it. There in the hallway with the door to his back, he lost control. He broke like a twig in the middle of a hurricane. All the years of holding back came out. "I'm sorry, I'm so sorry." In that moment the floor became holy ground. He bowed and prayed. He bowed and cried, "I'm sorry, I'm sorry."

Who was it that he apologized too? Was it God? Was it Janet? Was it his children? Was it the church membership? Maybe it was Sophie or even Jamaica. He didn't know. All he knew was his heart was breaking and his soul was damaged. So

much had happened so soon, and in that moment his life took a nosedive. "I'm sorry, I'm so sorry."

His body ached. He couldn't move. He didn't want to move. He found his bed on the floor and cried some more, pleading to an unknown spirit. Maybe he was begging mercy to all the people he had harmed. Maybe he was pleading with his own soul. Me, forgive me for making bad decisions. Me, forgive me, for living a life to please everyone but me. Me, forgive me, for being so confused and for living a lie. His body quivered from the chill of his tears. He was cold — too cold to move. Too tired to move. Too hurt to move.

The time ticked in the wrong direction. He wished the time could move backwards. Back to the day he decided to become a minister. Back to the day when he heard God say, "Preach." He wished he had said no. "I'm sorry God for wishing I had said no. You have been good to me, but this hurts so much. I'm afraid of what they will do, and I fear even more what I will do to me," he prayed.

His eyes remained closed. The shake of his body was comforted by a touch. A gentle touch that stroke his back and neck. It was Janet. She kissed his face as he cuddled in his tears. "I know you're hurting baby," her voice vibrated in an effort to mask her tears. "No matter what, know that I do love you."

"How can you love me after all I have done to you?" The words sounded like a confession.

"I love you because you have always loved me, Simon. I love you because you have a heart of gold. You have a love for God and for God's people. I love you because we have been to Hell and back together, and I will always love you because I care. No matter what I will always be your friend."

Simon turned to grab her. They embraced as if nothing had ever happened. They cried together for they knew that their love and their life together had been battered by the work of the church. They knew there was a love between the two of them that had been tarnished by the intrusion of God's people. They knew that both of them had made mistakes that had impacted their love. Simon wished he could turn back the clock. If he could, he would have built on his friendship with Janet.

"I'm not going to ask you about last night, Simon," Janet said calmly. Simon took a deep breath. A peace entered his spirit. "I'm not going to ask you not because I'm not hurt, but because it doesn't matter. You're going through a lot right now, and I don't want to add to your pain. What I have to tell you may make it worse. There again, it could make it better."

She squeezed him tight. "What I'm about to tell you isn't because you've hurt me. I'm not trying to get even. I'm long past that. I've come to recognize that I've been lashing out at you because of my own guilt. I've been blaming you for what I was guilty of. Do you understand, Simon?" He was surprised by her words. The last part penetrated a part of his consciousness that he forgot was there.

"Simon, I'm moving to Chicago at the end of this month. I've accepted a job teaching at the University of Chicago."

He did not know what to feel. Should it be anger, sadness, regret, fear, or relief? All of these emotions were bottled together. He was angry that the decision was made at such a bad time. He was sad that his marriage was coming to an end. He regretted that more wasn't done to stop the madness. He feared what would happen once the

people learned of this news. He was relieved that it was finally coming to an end.

"I've already found a school for the kids. We have to tell them. I thought it would be best if we'd tell them together." Simon wasn't ready for that. The thought of losing his children was more than he could take. He sobbed some more.

"How will I make it without my kids? Oh, God." He pushed away from Janet and cried alone.

"We'll have to figure out a way to make it work Simon. Chris and Carmen need you. I don't want them growing up without your active involvement in their life. We'll have to make it work. I'm sorry, but we have to make it work."

She was right. This was the only way.

"There's one more thing."

"What."

"I'm telling you because I think I should be the one to tell you. I may not be going alone." All of his male macho instincts came to the surface. "There's a chance that I may be going with a man. I've been seeing him for a year now."

"What!" Simon exploded. He knew he was in a bad place to judge. It didn't matter. He felt betrayed and deceived. He had many questions, but knew that if he asked them now she would ask about last night. He wasn't prepared for that.

"I have to tell you who he is Simon. I have to tell you because it may come back to you."

"Who is the nigger?"

"It's Maurice Burt."

"No! That jive nigger has been smiling in my face and fucking my wife behind my back?"

"He didn't know the connection between the two of us when we first met."

"So, once he found out, my friendship with him wasn't strong enough to make him stop? That's

cold." Simon was beginning to wonder who he could trust. Maurice had always stood in his corner. Now he didn't know if it was all a lie.

"I'm sorry Simon. I had to tell you. I feel bad about what has happened." He could tell that she was hurting. Something had changed in her voice. She didn't have to tell him. He knew she loved him. He knew she cared. She had taken a chance.

Simon reached out to hold her hand. "So, he's good to you?" He forced a smile. Maurice seemed to be a great guy. He could understand why she would be attracted to him. He had the looks that women loved. He wanted Janet to be happy, even if it meant with another man. "It's sounds serious. Do you love him?"

"I do."

"He's a lucky man. I'll miss you. I'm sorry for all I've taken you through. Do you know that?"

"It wasn't just you, Simon. Our marriage died a long time ago. We held on because of the church. It was only a matter of time before this happened."

"What about the power of God to change all things? Why didn't that work for us Janet?"

"Maybe it did. Maybe God changed all things. Maybe God created a way for us to become what we were supposed to be. I know that I'm a better person because of you, and that I will always love you. I know that your heart belongs to someone else. We can't make it into something it can't be."

"I hear you, but doesn't that go against what I preach?"

"Maybe. Maybe not. There comes a point in life when a person has to decide on what God is really saying. Is God what those people think? Is

God limited to a few words found on a few pages in an old book? Is the love of God ended when a person can't live up to the expectations of the people and that book? Should we put our lives on hold because the people want to brag about the first family of the church? Simon, I'm tired of living for God's people. It's time for us to live for God."

Janet had always been a wise woman. This was the type of conversation the two of them would have before they got married. They would sit and debate over theological issues for hours at a time. That seemed so long ago.

They talked until it was time to get the kids ready for school. Simon felt better. He never told her about last night. He didn't have to. She knew and he knew that all that mattered now was their friendship. That was something that would never die. They needed each other. Not in the way they had assumed. They needed the friendship that led to their marriage. They needed to know that nothing would rob them of the pleasure of having each other. Not even the sharing of their love.

•

Simon forced his way to work. He hadn't slept and the crying session on the floor had taken all of his remaining energy. He was tempted to not go in, but he didn't want to give the impression that he was defeated before the meeting.

He got there after 10:00 a.m. Sophie wasn't at her desk. It didn't surprise Simon that she wasn't there; in fact he was glad to have the opportunity to walk into his office without having to pretend nothing happened between the two of them the day before.

Simon had a number of things to get out of the way before the end of the week. Wednesday was his day to teach. He had a class at noon and

again at 7:00 p.m. Teaching came easy for Simon. The noon class was a more laid back session on the Old Testament. That evening he would teach from Paul's Epistle to the Romans. The good news was he didn't have to teach his class at the local divinity school. Each semester he taught courses in theology and substance abuse. It was spring break. He did have to grade mid-term exams. That would have to wait for another day.

He was struggling with his message for Sunday. He struggled because he wasn't sure there would be a need for a message. The meeting made it virtually impossible to determine what or if to preach. He believed in preparation. He wanted to do his best not to preach at the problems in the church. Some people criticized him for doing that, but he worked hard to keep himself out of the sermon.

He considered preaching a sermon on confronting chaos. The relevant questions were many. Why does chaos come? What does it take to remove the chaos? What do we do when we've done all we can and chaos is still there? Could it be that what we perceive to be chaos is nothing other than the presence of God? He reflected on the possible answers to these questions.

All he knew was his life had become chaotic. It was too much to consider at this point. He was fooling himself in thinking he could write a sermon at this point. He needed to unwind. The bad news was he couldn't. There was too much work to do not to continue to function. Like it or not, he had to write a sermon, and it had to be the sermon of his life.

Sophie finally arrived for work. His door was open. She walked by without saying good morning.

She didn't ask if he needed anything. She never explained why she was late. She went to her office and closed the door. The rest of her day was spent behind the door.

The office was quiet. It was the calm before the storm. No phone calls. No people walking in off the street in need of help from the church. No one stopped by to simply talk. No one came for counseling. No one came to complain or to support. It was God's gift before the storm. Simon needed time to reflect. He couldn't reflect. There were too many voices in his head.

There was something he had to do before it was too late. He picked up his phone. It rang three times. "Hello."

"Patsy, this is Simon." They hadn't talked since her last visit. "I was just checking to see how you're doing."

"I'm fine. The question is how are you?"

"To be honest, I've had better days. Things are really crazy right now."

"I know. I've been waiting for you to call."

"I've wanted to. You know that. It's just bad timing. I hope you understand."

"Of course I understand. That's why I wanted you to call. All I want is to be a safe place for you. I just want you to be happy."

"It's all so hard."

"Don't make it harder than it has to be. I'm safe. I won't hurt you. Do you know that?"

"Yes."

"So, why don't you let me take care of you?"

"Because I can't."

"Why not?"

"Because I'm your pastor."

"How long will you hide behind that? We have feelings for each other. We're two adults who

understand the game. All I want is to be your friend."

"I thank you for that, Patsy. I really do. Just let me get past this meeting. After that we can talk. Some things have come up. Some things that will change my life."

"Do you need anything?"

"You've given me everything I need. Thank you for that."

"I wish I could do more."

"Just pray for me and be my friend." He hung up the phone feeling better. He had run from Patsy since she came to his office. He did not know what to say. He wanted to keep the door open. He wasn't sure about what would happen. Maybe he and Patsy could get together after the dust settled.

There was one more call to make. "Hey, Jamaica." The afterglow was still in his voice.

"What took you so long to call me, big boy? You know I needed to hear your voice."

"I was still walking on the cloud and I got lost."

"You know you need help."

"No, girlfriend. I need you."

"So, does that mean I get to see you tonight."

"I can come by after Bible Study."

"That sounds good. So, how did it go this morning?"

"Better than I thought it would. Janet didn't go off on me. In fact she came with her own news."

"What?"

"She's leaving at the end of the month."

"You lying!"

"She took a job at the University of Chicago."

"How do you feel about it?"

"I'm okay. We had a nice talk. She told me she didn't need for me to tell her where I was because she was guilty."

"What do you mean?"

"She's been having an affair with one of the men at the church."

"You stop!"

"He may be going with her to Chicago. He just finished his MBA. The boy is ten years younger than her."

"I ain't mad at her for that."

"That's the thing. I couldn't be mad. I must admit that the thought of someone else screwing my wife didn't feel good."

"I can understand that."

"It helped me understand how she must have felt."

"Do you think it was revenge?"

"Maybe at first, but not now. I want her to be happy. That's all that matters. Maybe we can both move on with our lives now."

"What does that mean for you?"

"It means now I can move on what I feel for you," there was a long pause. "There's nothing stopping our being together."

"It sounds like we need to talk. We can do that when you come over tonight."

"That's cool."

There was so much to do and not a lot of time to get it done. Simon knew that the course of his life would be defined within the next 48 hours. He grieved the loss of his marriage, yet found comfort in what might emerge on the other side. This was his chance to become the man that was kicking on the inside to come out and play.

•

"Could it be that we have lingered in the wilderness for so long we have mistaken the wilderness for the Promised Land?" Simon asked his noon Bible Study group. "We have become comfortable in the wilderness. We plant lilies in the sand and wonder why they die. The heat of the sun beats on our back, leaving a constant reminder of where we are, and why we are where we are, yet, we call it a good day. We can't find any shade in the wilderness. No water to quench our thirst. Yet we think it's the Promised Land.

"Black folk, we're not in the promised land. We've been in the wilderness too long. We think we have overcome and we have settled down. The suburb is not the Promised Land. It's just a new improved version of the same old Hell. We've run from the ghetto streets yet take with us a slave mentality that continues to isolate and alienate those who are our brothers and sisters.

"We've moved up the corporate ladder and take home nice pay. We step out of our fancy cars parked in the garage attached to our nice home away from the crime of the inner city. We step into our utopian fantasy that is no other than a figment of our imagination. This is not the Promised Land. The Promised Land is over there. We've planted our lilies and built our houses in the wilderness, yet it will crumble because it ain't real.

"God did not bring us to this place to get comfortable. The journey isn't over, it just got started. We can't stop until everybody gets to the other side. We can't sing, 'It's me, it's me, it's me oh Lord' We have to sing, 'it's us, it's us, it's us oh Lord, sure enough standing in the need of prayer.' Yes it's my mother, it's my father, it's my brother, it's my sister, it's the crack addict down the street, it's the

prostitute on the corner, it's the molested child hiding in the back of the church, it's the battered wife hiding behind dark-shaded glasses, it's the confused child begging to be heard, it's the rough neck Negro who won't come to the church because God's people have become too holy to be any good. It's us, it's us, it's us oh Lord, standing in the need of prayer."

The small group stood and clapped. The amens filled the air. Simon was filling the spirit. His passion for real ministry came out near the end of his Bible Study. He couldn't help himself. Some people call it the anointing. Whatever it was, it felt good.

"Let's gather for prayer. God knows we need to pray. We need to pray that we regain our focus. We need to pray that the inner fighting come to an end and the real work of ministry will prevail. We need to pray that the stench of death that fills the air will be replaced by the smell of redemption. We need to pray that justice will roll down like the mighty waters, and the grace and peace will abound in this time of distress." Simon felt his need for prayer. He needed God's direction on what to do. His personal and his professional lives were on a collision course. Which would win this battle that was not just flesh and blood?

He asked Jessie, one of the associate ministers to pray. Jessie was a faithful participant in the noon Bible study. He prayed for the church. He prayed for the community. He prayed for himself. He prayed for his pastor. Everyone embraced at the end of his prayer.

"I love you, Pastor," Stan, another supporter, said. "You know I got your back. Whatever you do, I am behind you."

The others said the same. Hazel, an older member, took his hand. "I came to this church because I was hurting. You helped me overcome my hurt. I was addicted to prescription medication. You helped me with my pain. Now, I feel your pain. It's all over your face." She touched his face. "You're just a man. We put too much on you. Thank you Jesus! Oh I feel your pain!"

Stan, Jessie and Monica came to the rescue. "I feel his pain," Hazel continued. "We need to pray for our pastor. Can you'll feel his pain. It's too much for one man. It's too much!"

Simon kneeled in submission as the faithful prayed for him. They told God they loved him. They begged God to strengthen and heal him. They prayed for his marriage, his family, his ministry, his vision, and the people who fought against him. Each person prayed, one by one. They loved Simon. They believed in him. They could tell he was wounded. They stood in the gap.

Simon needed their love. It was times like these that kept him going. It was because of people like these that he stayed at Shady Grove. They needed him. Their lives had been changed because of the ministry he provided. He feared what would happen to the church if he left. He feared that the church would revert to its old ways. It would regress back to being a church like all other churches—content with providing service to those who are already in the church.

Simon was concerned about the unchurched. More specifically he worried about those who had never stepped foot in a church. So many had become disillusioned with contemporary church life. They were turned off by the fancy words coming from the pulpits and the begging for more money.

They desired a place of worship that took community action seriously. Simon was serious about the community. Many wanted him to be more serious about the people who were members of the church.

Membership didn't matter to Simon. Over the years he had stated that it's not biblical. "Why is it that Biblical literalist are so quick to point to the text that endorse their own agenda, yet refuse to accept those that contradict their assumptions?"

Simon did not apologize for being a liberal thinker. He challenged people to think for themselves. "The problem with people is they think the Bible is God. God is bigger than the Bible. If God has been reduced to everything written in the Bible, then we conclude that all there is to know about God is found on these pages. I don't know about you, but my God is bigger than that. My God is bigger than what can be recorded on a few pages. You may not like it, but you have limited God."

Comments like these kept him in trouble. He challenged the people not to judge others. "God has not called us to judge, but to love. The problem is we're too busy doing God's job, and we spend very little time doing our own."

"You have been fake for so long that you don't know who you are," he once preached. "You have structured your life to satisfy people you either don't know or don't like. It has become more important to you to please other people than to please God. Our goal should be to be so comfortable with who God has made us to be that we don't care about what people think about how we look. Imagine how much money you could save if you stopped pleasing people and started pleasing God. Would you need to spend all that money on those clothes you don't need? Could you have waited

before buying that car? Do you need to get your hair done every week? Say amen somebody."

He told them to be transparent. As the people prayed for him he remembered his own struggle.

•

The year was 1975. Simon was in the middle of his sophomore year in high school. It was the best of times. It was the time in-between not knowing and beginning to understand the meaning of it all. It was the time all people walk before entering that scary place—adulthood. It's the place where time wasted becomes regret, and future dreams seem too far to catch.

After a tough transition from grade school to middle school, and then from middle school, to high school, he finally felt like things were coming together. The missing piece was a social life. No girlfriend. No first kiss. No one to call his first love. No slow grinds to brag about or first glance at bare breasts to prove his true manhood.

His world was books and television. There was no time for girls and play. His skinny frame and thick glasses failed to attract girls. Simon was known for his brains. "See no evil, hear no evil, speak no evil," were the common chants of naughty kids. The chants no longer bothered him. All that mattered was the wonderful adventures that came from the books.

Simon was gaining a new reputation. During the previous year he started running track. He could run. Not well, but he could run. He learned to run out of fear. The neighborhood boys would chase him home chanting, "See no evil, hear no evil, speak no evil." Things were changing. His body was changing. His desires were changing. Deep down the words hurt, yet the hard exterior hid all

pain. Nineteen seventy-five was the year that changed everything.

Mom walked into the living room area with a different look on her face. He could tell that she had something to say. Something that would rock his world. Something that would change the way he viewed life, the way life treated him, and the way he viewed people.

Simon was in the middle of his evening routine. Study time was followed by a few hours of television. It was Friday night, and, unlike most boys his age, he didn't spend his weekends engaged in ruthless behavior. He was too shy and timid to go out and chase girls or party.

Sanford and Son was on the tube. Simon was inspired by the story of a black junk dealer. In retrospect it was quite pathetic that his role models were, to a large extent, those on television. Sadly, most of those role models were struggling blacks that made him laugh. What he needed was a story of a black family who prospered in white America.

Mom walked in during one of the funny scenes, "I'm comin' home Elizabeth," Redd Foxx mimicked after not getting his way from Lamont, his son. Mom came into the room in the middle of a big laugh.

There was a different look on her face. The look puzzled Simon. He had seen Mom down before. He had seen her cry. He knew what it looked like for her to be down, but this was a different look. It was a look that said, "Stop the press." This was the look of despair.

"Simon, I need to talk to you," she moaned. The sound of holding back parted her lips. The sound of holding back pain filled the air. He knew that sound. He had played that game many times. He had played being strong for other people. He

had pretended to be strong while holding back the tears. He knew that sound. It was the fake sound designed to conceal the angst of a suffering heart.

"What?" that's all he knew to say. He knew that Hell was about to break loose. He knew that something was coming that he didn't want to hear. Something that he would rather not hear. He knew that look. He knew that sound. He knew pain all too well.

"It's about Crystal," she began. Crystal had been to the doctor all day after dizzy spells. Simon had been waiting for Mom and Crystal to return from the doctor for over six hours.

"It ain't good. She has a tumor the size of an egg in her brain. The doctor says she may not make it," the pain came out. Her baby girl was dying. She stood in the middle of the room and cried uncontrollably leaving Simon with no words, no comfort, no place to go.

Why, God? That was the first thing to cross his mind. How could this happen to me? How could you, God, do this to my baby sister?

Simon had been conditioned to deal with his own pain, but he wasn't prepared to contend with this pain. This pain was beyond him. It was bigger than him. It was more than he could push to the side. He couldn't pretend that it would go away. How? Why? What? Questions filled his soul. Tears, once hidden, began to explode like the eruption of Mt. St. Helen.

He ran from the room leaving his mother alone in the middle of the floor to cry. Where to go? What to do? All defenses were gone. There was no room large enough for him to run to. No pillow large enough to soak his tears. No heroes to protect him.

After 25 minutes of forever, he ran from his room to the Hell that had been shielded from him for 15 years. For 15 years he ran from the darkness of the streets. That Friday night, darkness penetrated his world of innocence. Finally, after 15 years, he would be introduced to the world of shadows. This world of evil, this world of trickery and secrets would create in him a new identity.

He ran to the darkest corner—Dean Street and Banks Avenue. Dewayne was there. Dewayne possessed a special quality, a quality that Simon wished he had. He never seemed to show emotion. Never mad, glad, scared or afraid. He moved through life with an ease that Simon could only dream of having. His emotions changed like the weather. Some days hot, others cold, some stormy, some calm. Like the weather there was no way of predicting or controlling his emotions. Dewayne had something special. Simon hoped for a way to hide all emotions. He wanted the world of the fake and cruel. Simon walked into the world of the hard boys who scared people with their stare.

He was alone on the corner with a bottle in his hand. He was always alone. He didn't seem to mind. He would often laugh at himself for no apparent reason. The bottle was in his hand. He often carried a bottle or a pipe, and moved throughout the neighborhood—alone.

"What's up, Simon," a polite greeting slurred from his lips.

"Nothin' man. What ya doing," Simon didn't want to tell the truth. He was afraid that he would cry. He didn't want to tell him about his sister and her illness. He didn't want to talk about the large lump in his chest that felt like it would burst like a bubble at any moment. He needed something to cover the pain in his soul. The pain was too much

for pillows. The pillows of his yesteryears no longer helped quench his ache. Pillowcases knew his tears. They heard his cry after his run home from his lesson on becoming a man. The pillow against his face was his secret place to release the pain of not knowing why.

His secret world couldn't take away that lump in his chest. Simon needed something different, something stronger, something to take him away from the Hell of that moment. Something more than a pillow to scream into. More than a place to hide and wait for the pain to go away. This was the place of no hiding. There was no hiding place.

Dewayne took another swallow from his bottle. It looked like water, but Simon knew what it was. It was the same bottle hidden under the kitchen counter. That same bottle that Daddy brought out on every Friday night before he went to singing the blues. He would take it out on Friday and drink until Sunday.

There in the family room he would start his ritual—every Friday. B.B. King, Percy Sledge, Bobby Blue Bland, and others would visit the house on Friday. Friday was the day of the blues. Saturday was dedicated to Marvin and Aretha and others who made you swing. The beat of Rhythm and Blues would rivet through the house forcing all within earshot to shake their booty to the bass beat. Come Sunday morning, James Cleveland would sing, "Peace Be Still." It was time to get his soul right.

He would drink until his eyes were blood shot with the red of intoxication. There, in the family room, he would drink until the peace of sleep calmed the rage of the week. From Monday till

Friday he would work like a burdened mule in Masta's field. From sunrise to sunset and beyond, his father would work. He worked and slept, worked and slept, worked and slept. And then, on the weekend, he drank and sang the pain away.

"Can I have a drink," Simon begged. It worked for his father. Certainly it would work for him.

Did he really want a drink? He hated the way it smelled. He hated what it did to his father. He hated the thought of what it might do to him. Did he really want a drink? Deep down a voice said no. Deep down a voice said yes. This is what Paul meant when he talked about the struggle between good and evil, flesh and spirit, God and the Devil.

Dewayne looked at Simon like a man who had hit the lottery. This opportunity to corrupt the neighborhood good boy seemed to be what he needed to bring joy into his meaningless existence. He smiled. It was the smile of evil. The glare in his eyes reminded Simon of those pictures of the devil in Sunday school books.

"Yeah man, have a drink," he slurred as the smell of intoxication filled the air.

It was Puerto Rican rum. The hard stuff. Clear as water. Deadly as rat poison. Simon looked at the bottle—100% alcohol. He thought what does that mean. Does that mean 100% satisfaction? Does that mean 100% agony?

Simon closed his lips around the bottle. It smelled bad. He closed his eyes and thought, Crystal has cancer. She may die. He wanted to cry. He was afraid to cry. He needed to cry. Instead of crying he swallowed. He swallowed long and hard. He swallowed until his head swirled. He swallowed until he forgot where he was. He swallowed until the rum numbed his pain.

He looked up at the streetlights. They were bright. Suddenly the street came to life. The sound of dogs barking, the sound of cars passing by, the sound of kids playing three houses from where he sat—sounds filled his ears. Lights and sounds. Lights and sounds never before noticed suddenly took hold of his life. A world never before known became his new hiding place.

Lights and sounds, dogs barking and children playing, passing cars and a spinning world all replaced the pain of what Momma said—"Crystal has cancer. She may not make it." The fear went away. It felt good. Simon needed this escape. He needed a world distant from Momma's words. He needed a world where he could forget the pain of the penis in his face. A place where he could forget all the childhood memories locked away in the secret closets of his conscience.

The rum helped him forget. It created for Simon a place where he didn't have to think about not crying. Instead of crying he tripped on the lights, the children, the dogs, the cars, the stars, the world became a place to laugh at. The rum did that for him.

With each swallow it was easier taking the next. With each sip the taste and smell got easier to take. After swallowing half the bottle Simon knew that he could never go back. He liked it too much to go back. He could never go back to being the weak punk who did all the right things. He could never be the bookworm again. With each swallow he became more street savvy.

It felt like he was going up. Simon didn't know that he was going down. Down, down, down. With each day that followed for the next two years he would go down, down, down. With each

swallow came the desire for more. More rum, more weed, more cocaine, more acid, more heroin. More, more, down, down, down he went with each passing day.

They drank, Dewayne and Simon, until the rum was gone. They sat there on the street corner laughing at their surroundings.

"Man you alright when you get that stick out your ass," Dewayne giggled after yet another swallow. "I thought you was nothin' but a punk ass. Shit man you alright when you put them fuckin' books down."

Simon was happy to hear those words. He had struggled with trying to fit in. He tried fitting in by reading books, and sharing information with people. That never worked; in fact it made it even more difficult for him to fit in. He tried being cool, but that never worked. He only made more of a fool of himself. He couldn't walk the walk. He couldn't talk the talk. Simon simply lacked the stuff that made one cool. In his hand was the key to being cool. The rum enabled him to talk that jive. Dewayne saw what no one had seen before—Simon was a cool nigger.

"I ain't no punk, man. I play that game for my parents. Shit, man, I ain't no punk," he said that word. He said shit. The words staggered off his lips. They came out like a fearful rat long caged in but afraid of being set free. He tried more, "What the fuck you know 'bout me, man?" The second time was easier than the first. Shit, fuck, motherfucker, punk ass jive turkey, it was easier, like the rum, with each word uttered.

"What ya doin' tomorrow man," Dewayne asked. The boys from the street hadn't asked Simon that.

"Nothin' man. Why?"

"Me, Hawkeye and the boys gonna hang. Ya wanna come?" Simon wanted to say yes. He wanted to say no. He was afraid of Hawkeye. Hawkeye was a tough dude from the projects. He hung with a gang of boys known for staying in trouble. Simon knew that he should ask his mother. He knew that he couldn't ask his mother. He felt himself getting bold. He was going down. Down, down, down.

"Yeah man. Count me in."

"Alright. Meet me at the park," Dewayne gave Simon the soul brother shake, and walked away leaving him intoxicated, bewildered, yet at peace. Momma's words no longer haunted him. His eyes were heavy. His legs were wobbly. He struggled to stand up. As he stood he laughed at himself. He laughed because he was behaving like the old drunks he watched on television.

A step and stumble. Step and stumble. Step and stumble. Home was so far away. The one block walk back to 309 Dean Street took him longer than his walk to the corner. Step, stumble, laugh, fall, step, stumble, laugh, fall.

The porch light was on. All lights were off on the inside. It was after midnight. Simon had never been out this late before. If he had, his mom would have come out to wup his ass. The fear of what she would do had been enough to keep him home. Home safe from the world of street demons. He was going down.

He staggered to the door doing his best not to make too much noise. Simon didn't want Mom to see him drunk. He pressed his head against the door and spread his legs to keep from falling as he dug deep into his pocket for his keys. Finally, he found them. Finding the right key was a task.

Getting the key in the door and unlocking the door was even harder. Finally, he opened the door.

His dog, Fluffy, greeted him with an unending bark. "Ruff, ruff, ruff." Simon wanted to step on him to shut him up. He tiptoed to the bathroom. Something was wrong with his stomach. Something felt like it was coming up. His stomach rumbled like a locomotive. Hurry up. Hurry up, his head said. No, no his body responded.

It was less than 20 feet to the bathroom. It felt like a long distance run in the middle of the summer. The bathroom was across from his mother's bedroom. Good! The door was closed. He barely made it in time. Vomit exploded from his gut. Each swallow came out. The taste of the rum crossed his lip. It came out everywhere. In the toilet, on the toilet, on the floor, in the sink, on his shoes, on his shirt. Vomit was everywhere. The smell of vomit was everywhere. It wouldn't stop coming.

It was painful. It was loud and painful. Still no sound from his mother's bedroom. Still no knock on the bathroom door. His head was spinning. He couldn't think. He stood up. Too early, more vomit. He stood up again. His arm hit the light switch.

"Help," he cried. The darkness frightened him. He thought he had gone blind. Simon didn't know what to do. The darkness left him not knowing what to do. He tried to get out. He couldn't find the door. He stumbled and fell. He fell into the bathtub. His head hit the wall. It felt like he was bleeding, but he couldn't tell. It was too dark.

Simon couldn't move. He didn't want to move. He tried but he couldn't. The walk to the house, and the pressure of getting to the bathroom was too much for him to endure. He closed his eyes

and slept. He slept in a puddle of vomit in the bathtub. He slept with the whiff of intoxication in the air. He slept because he had nothing else to do. He couldn't move or think. There in the bathtub he slept afraid that he had gone blind.

He had gone blind. It was hard to stop after the first drink. With that first drink a world once unknown was unlocked. With that drink came more drinks. With it, came a new interest — girls. Being cool came with that first drink. Fitting in and getting over came with that drink. That drink changed his life. He became a man, with that drink. Or could it be he lost his manhood, with that first drink?

See no evil, hear no evil, speak no evil was lost that night. Staying home on Friday nights was never to be seen again. He learned a new talk, a new walk, and developed a new attitude. The hair changed. The clothes changed. He found a new walk — they called it a pimp. Simon learned to cuss and to play the dozens. Fighting became something he looked forward to, rather than something to fear.

Why these changes? Life didn't matter. The next day no longer mattered. The books no longer provided solace, instead they added to the trauma. The fantasy world on those pages revealed a world of hypocrisy and division. It was the white man's world. The things on those pages did not belong to him.

How does one end up at rock bottom? One drink leads to another. Another to yet another. Before you know it, things are out of control. Before you know it, you are unable to resist the unyielding temptation of the bottle.

The bottle led to marijuana. From marijuana, Simon graduated to cocaine. From cocaine to acid. From acid to heroin. It never was enough. That's

how a person ends up in the bottom. You get there without knowing you're on a journey. It's a trip loaded with sleeping travelers. No one wants to end there. No one wants to die, but they do.

They get there because of pain. The hole in the soul becomes too big to fill with love, joy, peace, compassion, amusement—no emotion satisfies the deep hurt in a person headed on a journey to the bottom. Everyone there is surprised. They all thought they would be satisfied with one hit, one drink, one night of pleasure. None expected dependency.

Soon, nothing else matters. To Hell with the books. Forget what Mamma says. Daddy's whip no longer controlled the rage. It was Simon's thang, and he was doing what he wanted to do. Why not? Nothing else made sense. No one else seemed to understand the pain hidden deep within—not even himself.

•

Simon couldn't forget where he came from. It was the cause of the passion that led him to ministry. It was the fuel that made him keep going. It was the reason for his being. He craved the satisfaction of helping a person find recovery. Like him, there were countless men and women on the streets who had given up on themselves because of pain. Some understood. Many didn't.

The people who prayed for him had been touched by his approach to ministry. They knew there would be a shootout on the next day, and that their pastor and friend may not survive the struggle. They would be left with no place to go. No place to feel comfortable. They would be forced to conform to a theological understanding that they had learned not to accept. They had been taught to look deeper into the text. To consider the culture and history of

the people the text was written. They had been taught to ask what the text says to the people of this age, and what it says to them personally. They were told that the purpose of the text might be different for God's people today, but that it still has validity.

They prayed because their pastor was hurting because of God's people, and because they were hurting because their way of thinking was under attack. This had become a war of approaches and they were caught in the middle.

•

Simon and Janet decided to tell the kids after school. Simon picked up Chris and Janet picked up Carmen. They met at Goodberry's for ice cream. Both knew how traumatic a separation and divorce could be on children. Even more tragic would be the impact caused by the change in environment. They would move to a new house, leave their friends and church, and all they had come to love. They would be a long distance from their father. That would be hardest on Carmen, the youngest child.

"How was school today," Janet spoke to break the ice.

"Same as always. Dull as heck." Chris said. He claimed he was bored and needed to be put up a grade to challenge is advanced mind. It had become the subject of much debate.

"I wonder what Einstein did when he got bored?" Simon countered.

"It sure wasn't buying new clothes. Did you know he wore the same thing everyday?" Chris said. "He did that because he didn't want to waste any time thinking about what to wear."

"That's stupid," Carmen said. At 10 she had already taken up a fascination for fashion. "It

sounds to me like he was just lazy." Everyone laughed.

"Well, I have some good news and some bad news," Janet decided it was time to put everything on the table. "I found a school that will except you at an advanced level. You will begin next year a grade higher."

"Yeah boy! That's what I'm talking about. Recognize the mind," Chris shouted as he gave his sister a high five.

"The bad news is the school is in Chicago," Janet waited for a response.

"What? That's a long way," Carmen said. "I don't want to go to Chicago."

"I have to go there baby. Mommy has a new job teaching at the University of Chicago. It's what I've always wanted."

"It will be good for your mother. I know it's a long way, but it will be good for you too," Simon did his best to support the move. The best thing for the kids was to see the two of them working together. They had to be a team; otherwise the kids would be lost.

"There's bad news," Simon felt he needed to say the rest. Janet had done her part. It was his turn to share the rest. "I won't be going to Chicago. I'll be staying here, or I may move somewhere else, but I won't be going with you."

"Why, Daddy?! Why?" both Carmen and Chris jumped in at the same time.

"Your mother and I have decided not to be together. We have also decided that our not being together does not mean that we will not be a family. We still love each other. We really love you. Our family will look a little different, but it's still a family. Do you understand?"

"No!" Chris blurted. "Why can't you and Mom stay together?"

"There are many reasons for that, Chris," Janet said. "We do love each other. We will always be friends, but we won't be together like we have been."

For the next 45 minutes Janet and Simon did their best to answer every question. They took their time. Some of the questions they didn't have answers to. The only thing that counted was their commitment to support their children. There was no need for them to suffer because of adult issues. They knew it wouldn't be easy, but they were willing to make it happen.

Simon remembered the day his mother left his father. He remembered something was wrong with Momma. She was more tense than usual. She came to school in a taxicab. The back seat was packed with bags. Crystal and Sandra were already in the taxi.

"Get in boy," she ordered.

"Where we goin' Momma," He asked. It was only 10:00 in the morning. They hadn't completed their first recess. Simon hadn't eaten lunch yet. He wasn't sick. He wondered, why is she getting me out of school early?

"We have to go to the Laundromat," was her answer. Simon couldn't figure out why. Why go to the Laundromat in the middle of the day? Why was she in a taxicab? Why were their clothes in luggage instead of laundry baskets?

They all packed in the cab like sardines. Momma, the cabdriver and Simon in the front seat. The bags, Sandra and Crystal in the back seat. Crystal sat on Sandra's lap to make room for all the bags.

His mother whispered something to the cab driver, as he turned left on Sexton Road. From there he turned onto Worley Street. Less than five minutes later he pulled in front of a blue house on Worley Street. This was not the Laundromat, Simon thought to himself. He knew this place. It was the home of one of his mother's friends. He knew the woman and the place, but had never been inside. His father didn't like this woman. Simon remembered the late night screams between his father and mother where the woman's name was mentioned. This woman was a bad influence on his mother. That's what Simon's father said.

Looking over her shoulder his mother quickly got her children out of the cab. "Take this bag boy and go inside."

The house was strange to Simon. An older woman with a rag on her head greeted them at the door.

"Ya'll come on in," she said with a sad look on her face. "Come on in, everything gonna be alright."

Simon's mother and older sister, Sandra, were behind Simon with bags in their hands. The bags from the back seat had been pulled out. They took all they had inside.

"Ya'll go outside and get the bags out of the trunk," his mother demanded; her voice pressing them to hurry as if someone might be looking. More bags, Simon thought. How much laundry do we need to wash?

The trunk was packed with bags. It seemed like everything they all owned was in the cab. Simon was confused. Why are we stopping here? Who is this woman? Why are we in a cab? So many questions with no answers. He was afraid to ask.

Once inside his mother and the woman went upstairs, leaving Crystal, Sandra and Simon to watch television. Time passed. Hours passed. They watched game shows. They watched *Days of Our lives*, and *Another World*—his mother's two favorite soap operas.

"It's time to go. Get up," his mother said, frightening Simon as his eyelids began to shut in preparation of much needed rest. It was after 4:00 in the afternoon. Crystal was cuddled next to him on the couch. Sandra was asleep on the floor in front of the television. She had been watching the soap operas. She was old enough to appreciate what they were about. To Simon and Crystal they were only about a bunch of white people talking about nothing.

They were all dazed by the activities of the day. Hurriedly, they transferred their bags into another taxicab. It seemed harder getting things in, than it had getting them out. By now all of Simon's energy was drained from sitting and watching television.

Crystal slept in Sandra's lap in the back seat. Again, Simon sat in the front seat with his mother. They traveled west on Worley, toward the downtown district. Traffic was beginning to pick up as people headed home after their shift at the hospital. School was out, and many kids were out walking the streets. A crowd was gathered at Douglas Park to play some street ball. You could hear the roar of the crowd after a good play. A slam dunk, or blocked shot.

Simon had never been to Douglas Park. His mother warned him not to go. The park was known for its shady activity. Alcohol, drugs, gambling, and

fighting. The park was so bad that it was rumored that the police were afraid to go there.

As they passed the park, Simon noticed two police cars in the parking lot at Jefferson Junior High School. The officers in the cars watched the activity at the park from a distance. Close enough to see, too far to do anything.

The park was the one section of town ruled by black folks. People in the 'hood took pride in it being a place that white folks were afraid of. That way they didn't have to worry about intrusions. The park was their place. A white person would be taking their life into their own hands if they ventured into the park.

Simon was scared of the park. His mother had spent so much time convincing him not to go, that he developed a fear of his own people. He feared the projects. The niggers over there were a different breed — at least that's what he thought. Without realizing it, Simon had developed the same opinion of his people held by many whites in the city. He feared them for no other reason than their color.

Simon had long given up on going to the Laundromat. All he wanted was a burger and fries. They had eaten a bowl of chicken noodle soup between *Days of Our Lives* and *Another World*. He needed more than soup. He craved McDonald's.

He wasn't alone. Sandra and Crystal were hungry too, but none of them had the guts to ask. Money was tight, and they knew better than ask to go to McDonald's. Eating out was a luxury. The gift of eating out was the family tradition that came when everybody was happy. This wasn't one of those days. Something was wrong. Silence dominated the day. Asking for McDonald's would be dangerous.

The taxicab turned left on Broadway. They were now in the heart of downtown. Downtown was the great divide in Columbia, Missouri. It divided the black community from the college community. Columbia was known for one thing. Everything in the city revolved around the students. The University of Missouri, Columbia College, and Stephens College were all positioned around the downtown area. The University of Missouri north of downtown, Stephens College just east of downtown, and Columbia College south of the downtown business district.

The downtown was designed with students in mind. Everyone else was just in the way. The black community was in the way. White college students pranced from shop to shop without a care in the world. Less than two blocks away was a community on the verge of eruption, and no one seemed to care. All that mattered, it seemed, was keeping students happy.

Simon watched the rich white students as they came out of the stores with bags in their hands. They came out of stores he had never been to. They weren't there for Simon and his family. The university wasn't there for him. It was there for the white kids from across the state. They came during the school year, leaving the streets bare during the summer.

The taxicab stopped in front of the Greyhound bus station. The Laundromat was on the other side of town. Simon was confused, tired and hungry, but knew better than to ask questions. The cab driver took his mother's money, opened the trunk, pulled out all their bags, and left them standing.

"Ya'll stay right here. I'll be right back," his mother ordered. She was on a mission. They knew it. The three tired and hungry children stood in front of a bus. People began to board the bus. Sandra, Crystal and Simon looked at each other, hoping someone would speak.

The trip was long and quiet. Simon's mother never told them where they were going, or why. "Next stop, Kirksville," the bus driver shouted.

"Not again," Simon whispered. Yet another stop on what felt like a journey to the gates of Hell.

"We'll be there soon," his mother promised. Simon wondered where there was, and why they were going there, and how long they would be there.

The trip lasted through the night. Crystal slept in Simon's arms. Mother and Sandra sat behind Simon and Crystal. The bus kept going. Every so often they would get off to eat, or use the bathroom, but not for long.

Finally, they reached their destination. Des Moines, Iowa. Some strange man was at the bus stop to pick them up. He drove them to an old brick house. Simon still had questions. He was too tired to ask, and he wouldn't have if he weren't tired. All he wanted was a warm bed. His body ached from the long drive.

"This is home," the man said as he parked behind the building. It was an old apartment building. "Ya'll staying upstairs," he continued.

Simon helped him get their things out of the car. The bags seemed heavier than when they first put them in the cab. His mother led the way up the stairs. The building was old. The floors creaked. Simon hated that. He wanted to go home. Why were they here? Simon hated it. He missed his Daddy. What was this all about?

"Come here boy," the man demanded. "I got something to show you." He led Simon into the bathroom. It smelled like old urine. "You the man of the house now boy. Let me show you how to take care of the toilet."

The man pulled the top off the toilet. "When you need to flush the toilet do it from here. You need to learn how to take care of this stuff because you in charge now boy. Your Momma and sisters need for you to be a man, and a man has to know how to take care of things. You hear me boy," he said.

"Yes sir," Simon responded. His emotions were mixed. On the one hand he was proud to be able to take care of his Momma and sisters. On the other, he didn't want to be the man. He wanted to go home and play. The thought of having to be the man of the household scared him to death. He didn't know this man. He didn't know where he was, and he didn't know why. All he knew was he wanted to go home.

What did it mean to be a man? Once again, a man, a family friend, gave instructions on being one. Could this man be trusted, or was he another mean man waiting to pull out his penis to be stroked and sucked? Was this man a friend or foe, protector or perpetrator? Simon listened in search for more than this man, his mother, or the strange new world he found himself trapped in were able to provide.

The next few months were unbearable. His mother did her best to make a life for her three children in Des Moines. The girls would play with their paper dolls, and Simon did the best he could to find meaning out of the Hellhole called his new home, but he detested it. He missed his friends, and his room. More than anything he missed his Daddy.

He grew to hate the strange man who came over from time to time to keep him company. He hated him for attempting to take the place of his father. His name eluded Simon. He was a waste of Simon's time, and he wished, every night, that he would go away.

He learned to appreciate hot dogs and pork and beans. Simon vowed never to eat another hot dog if God would rescue him from this dreadful existence. He wanted his father to show up. He never did. He prayed at night, "Please God, send my Daddy to take us away from this place."

Simon didn't understand why his father wouldn't come get them. Had he forgotten them? It wasn't like him not to be there for them when they needed him. They were struggling in making the ends meet. Why wasn't Daddy there to help them? No, things hadn't been perfect back in Columbia, but they were certainly much better than in Des Moines. They needed Daddy, but no one else seemed to see that.

Simon would ask about him, but his mother was quick to change the subject. Crystal was too young to understand, and Sandra had her own issues. Simon was the only one in the family who seemed to care that things had gotten out of control.

The other question being processed in his mind was even more painful than the first. Why was his mother doing this to them? Didn't she care that they had a life back in Missouri that was now torn asunder by this insane move to Hell. If she loved them, Simon thought, why would she do this to them? Why did she do this? Something had gone bad, and Simon was caught in the middle.

Things were progressively getting worse in Iowa. The heat of the summer was worsened by no air conditioner or fan. They did their best to stay

cool, but failed miserably. Ice cubes and popsicles didn't work. Late night cold baths and play in the shade didn't help.

You get irritable when you're hot. Sandra, Crystal and Simon snapped at each other for the silliest of reasons. Simon was at a disadvantage. He was the only boy, and the girls had girl things to do. He was left alone to play. There were no boys his age to play with, and his mother wouldn't allow him to venture out to meet new friends. Simon was glad. They were in a rough neighborhood, and his mother had warned him not to play with boys from neighborhoods like the one where he now lived.

It was different than Dean Street. There were no back yards to play in, no neighbors to talk to, no girls to talk about. Life in Des Moines was getting harder and harder. The heat made it tough. The wait made it even tougher.

Simon continued to wait for his father. He had no comprehension as to how far away they were. At first he assumed his father knew their whereabouts. One day it finally hit. He didn't know. He couldn't, otherwise he would have rescued them.

Simon made up his mind. He would call his father and tell him to pick them up. They didn't have a phone. Simon planned their rescue. He would take a dime from his mother's purse, and call collect from a pay phone. He waited for the right time. He would sneak out and run around the corner and make the call at the pay phone. He would do it while his mother cooked dinner. She wouldn't miss him. She would be too busy to notice.

The day came. He prepared to make his move. The sky was black. In a matter of minutes

the weather changed. The wind was fierce. He couldn't go now. It was too dangerous. There was a loud sound. It was the sound of a train.

"Oh my God," his mother screamed. "Come on kids," she grabbed Crystal. Sandra ran outside, Crystal and his mother were behind her. The sound of a siren filled the air. As Simon ran as quickly as he could, he looked over his shoulder. In the distance he saw it. A tornado.

His mother knocked on the door of a neighbor. He was in a basement apartment. "Please, can we come in," she begged. He opened the door. They were saved from the massive destruction outside. All night Simon contemplated his next move.

"I can't take anymore," he wept. "Why is this happening to me? I want to go home," he murmured to himself. He cried all night in a stranger's apartment. He couldn't sleep. He was too scared to sleep.

The next day Simon made that call. He called his father collect, and begged him to come get them. He did.

Simon knew things were bad for his mother and father, but he never thought it would come to this. Separation and divorce had never crossed his mind. Despite the insanity in his family, they had a way of working things out, for better or worse. That's the way things worked back in the '60s. You fought a little, you left, and you came back home as if nothing happened.

We talk about how things have changed. To a large extent this is true. Couples don't stay together like they used to, but it's not because they didn't have problems back then. The opposite is true. They had problems, but there weren't as many

avenues of escape for women who had become dependent on their husbands.

Simon was a suffering boy, not because his mother left his father, but because his mother left his father without helping him through the process. Simon was hurting because he didn't understand. The answer to his mother's pain was not for her to run away in fear, but to leave gracefully. Simon needed to maintain contact with his father. He didn't need to hear that he was the man of the household without being told that they were running away from his father.

Some argue that the children matter more than anything. Now, Simon was forced to deal with the same issues in his own marriage. When faced with what his mother faced, Simon understood for the first time what she felt that day on the bus. She, like Simon, wanted to stay for the children, but had to leave for her own sanity. Sometimes a short-term break is enough to heal the wounds. But there are those times when a person must break the chains of those who strap them.

The problem with what Simon's mother did was not her leaving. It's how she left. Simon still needed his father. He deserved the right to be with the man he idolized. His dad was his role model. He couldn't imagine what life would be like without his father. Simon needed his leadership. Without knowing it, his father was teaching him how to become a man.

Simon feared making the same mistake with his children. They would need their father. He would do his best to protect them from the pain he felt after his mother took him on that long trip to a Laundromat.

•

Simon couldn't wait for the end of the evening Bible Study. Many in the crowd wanted to meet with him to discuss their personal problems. They needed guidance to help them make it through the week. Normally, Simon would take the time to speak to each person. This night was different. Jamaica would be leaving the next day, and he didn't want to waste any time.

The room was dark with candles when he walked in. She wore a black thong and black high-heeled shoes. Simon had mentioned to her his fascination with high-heeled shoes. He loved the look of her ass in a thong. She knew how to get his attention. Nothing else needed to be said.

She didn't want to waste time on the small talk. The stage was set for lovemaking. He didn't ruin the moment. He took her in his arms and made love to her. They picked up where they left off the night before. There was no time to make it to the bed. There in front of the door, on the floor, they made love.

After they finished he lifted her in his arms and carried her to the bedroom. Not a word had been spoken. Their bodies said it all. His body said I love you. Hers said I need you. They took their time. For the first time they had no fear of being found out by Janet. For the first time, he was emotionally free to be with Jamaica. No fear of what would be said when he came home. No regard for not calling home to make sure everything was all right. Simon knew and Janet knew that everything was settled. It was time for both of them to move on. He felt free and at peace.

"Tell me what you thinking," Simon asked. These were the first words spoken since he arrived.

"I was thinking about how much I'm going to hate not being with you tomorrow night. I wish I could be with you."

"Me too. I wish you could be there."

"I was thinking about how good it's been over these past few days. It's like we've been together forever," Jamaica said. "You often wonder if what you feel for a person when you first meet is real. When you find them again after years of being apart and what you feel is the same, no, what you feel is even better, you know it must be real."

"I know. That's the way I feel," Simon said as he touched her face and sighed. "So, why don't we make it happen Jamaica? Why not find a way to be together?"

"What will that look like Simon?"

"It looks like two people loving each other and making it work."

"There's more to it than that."

"How much more can there be?"

"Don't get me wrong, Simon, I want to be with you. I really do. I've been thinking about this since you called. After all these years, Janet is walking away. It's our chance to make it happen. But..."

"But what?" Simon didn't like the way things were going. He sat up in the bed and changed the position of her head placing it in his lap.

"I'm not ready to be with a person who is a pastor. Look at what it did to you and Janet. Look at what it's doing to you. I can't let that happen to me. I love you Simon, but I can't deal with the life you live. I can't take the stress and heartaches that you deal with. I can't endure the constant nagging of so-called godly people. I can't adjust my life to conform to what they expect. I just can't."

"I'm not expecting you to be what they want you to be. I need you to be what I need. I don't care about how they expect you to dress or act. That doesn't matter to me."

"I know, but it will matter to them, and because it matters to them it will have an impact on us. I can't live a life in a glass house. The bricks will hurt me more than you. I'm not as strong as you. I'm afraid I can't take it."

"So, what happens next?"

Jamaica sat up next to Simon. "What's next is you'll come to Dallas to see me soon. What's next is I'll come see you. We'll see each other the way we are now as long as we can. I'm not ready to walk away, Simon. I'm just not ready to give you my all. I'm scared of what will happen to us when the wolves find out. Do you understand?"

Simon did understand. He understood that his life was filled with confusion and that not everyone was prepared to jump into the ship. Jamaica was smart enough to see what many are too blind to see. The life that comes with dating a person in ministry can be grueling. She was not ready to expose her life to the venom of the snakes in the pews. Simon couldn't blame her for that. He respected her honesty.

They made love again. It was his last chance to release all the pain before the meeting the next day. Tomorrow he would stand before an angry mob. Janet would not be there. Jamaica would not be there. For the first time Simon realized that he would be alone. Many supported him, but did not know him. He would stand before the jury and judge represented by no human council. He prayed for God's protection. He would need it because he felt alone.

Chapter Five – Thursday

"And Ezekiel saw a valley of dry bones"

FOR THE SECOND CONSECUTIVE DAY, Simon went to work without sleeping the night before. It had become a bad habit. Sleepless nights were the consequence of worry, fear, doubt, and anticipation. For these two nights he didn't sleep because of his desire to be with Jamaica. He couldn't sleep with her in the same room. She gave him energy. He wasn't tired. That was until he drove up to the church.

The first thing he did after entering his office was to check his voice mail. There was a stack of messages on his desk. People were waiting for a return call. He was too drained to answer them all. They would have to wait for another day.

Sophie called in sick. That didn't surprise him. He expected that she'd be out looking for a new job. He planned to ask her to resign after the meeting. He couldn't function knowing that she felt the way she did. He wanted to help her progress beyond her feelings, but he wasn't able to help her with her feelings.

He still hadn't completed Sunday's sermon. No text, no theme, no key points. Nothing. It was Thursday and time was running out. He picked up his Bible to read. He turned to Ephesians 5. He read out loud, "Take no part in the unfruitful works of darkness, but instead expose them. For it is a shame even to speak of the things that they do in secret, but when anything is exposed by the light it becomes visible, for anything that becomes visible is light. Therefore it is said, 'Awake, O sleeper, and arise from the dead, and Christ shall give you light.'"

He closed his Bible and his eyes. "Could I be the problem, Lord?" he prayed. "Is it because of me that the church is experiencing this trauma? Is it me that needs to be exposed to the light? Is it my love for Jamaica that kindles your judgment? Is it the pain of my marriage that stirs the contempt of your people, and are you behind all of this?"

Simon was beginning to wonder if it was his entire fault. "Are the critics right, God? Is my way of thinking too radical for your people? Is it because of me? Show me? Teach me? Scold me, forgive me."

He bowed in meditation. In the silence he only heard, 'wait.' Wait to see what happens next. Waiting had become the theme of his life. For the past two years Simon had waited on God to either confirm his need to stay, or to show him an exit from Shady Grove. Many told him to stay. Others told him to leave. It was getting harder for him to discern the voice of God. He sat and prayed.

His guilt of being with Jamaica was reduced after hearing Janet's confession. It was still wrong, but he felt justified by her actions. It was a silly argument given his action preceded his knowledge of Janet's affair. It didn't matter. He wanted to make it right. Deep down he knew it was wrong.

He couldn't accept it as wrong. He wanted to believe that God approved of his affair. He needed that validation to stand confident. It didn't help. The text reminded him that darkness shall come to the light.

He considered what his life would be like after Janet left. He knew many would contend that a divorce meant he could never marry again. He had heard this argument many times. He never thought that he would be forced to adjust his position to respond to the Biblical literalists in his church. He knew of the double standard between ministers and other people. Although many of the members had been married more than once, it didn't matter. It didn't matter because in their opinion the pastor is to live above the problems they live with every day.

He knew that dating would be a problem. He could not be seen in public places. He could not date anyone in the church. He could not date anyone who failed to fit the mold set by the people. She would have to dress the way they wanted, talk the way they wanted. They would want to approve of her. They would tell him if she was good enough, and they would chastise him if she failed to meet their expectations. They wouldn't consider how she made him feel, they would be more concerned about how she made them look. Did she know the church? Could she teach the children? What kind of personality did she have? Was she light skinned or dark? Did she have kinky hair or straight? Where did she go to college? Where does she work?

Simon knew it was coming because he had seen it happen to other ministers. Not only that, he saw it happen with Janet. He would have to contend with the women coming after him. He

would be approached in a different way. He knew that. He also knew that new rumors would come with his single status. If he dated women and dropped them after determining they weren't the one for him, he would be labeled a dog. If he refused to date until the right woman came along, they would say he's gay.

He would be forced to travel to date. He would have to make certain they weren't crazy before he took them out. Not every woman is prepared for the drama that comes with being with a man like him. He had a lot to consider. How long should he wait before he dated? What is appropriate? He could go to the movies, but not a jazz club, lunch but not dinner, a play but not a concert. What are the rules?

Simon contemplated telling the people about the break up at the meeting. Would it be too much to bring up given everything else that might come up? He decided to play it by ear. He wasn't sure if he wanted to stay. It was best to take it one step at a time, instead of jumping to a conclusion based on a variety of unknowns. It was enough to drive a man mad. Simon tried not to think about it all, but he had to. He had to because it was his reality and it wasn't going anywhere anytime soon.

Then there's Jamaica. The conversation from the previous night was the same as before. The same reason was given for their not being together. It was his work that got in the way of building a long-term relationship. Jamaica was different from most black women. It wasn't important to her that she land a big time preacher. She wasn't a child of the church. She rarely attended church. She was more in tuned with things of the spirit than the life of the church.

Like Simon, she read books regarding other world religions. She loved the compassion of Buddha, and studied Native American spirituality. She appreciated the teachings of Yoruba, and from time to time would meet with members of the Unitarian Universalist Church. She had read all of the works of Howard Thurman. She believed in God, but did not limit God to the way God is worshipped in black churches across the country.

The two had talked about emotional worship services, and how they distracted people from the teaching. She loved the music, but would rather listen to it at other times. When she went to church she wanted to hear a message that challenged people to be socially aware. She wanted to move the world beyond the restrictions. Homophobia had to be ended in the church before it could be shot down in the rest of the world. Christians would have to appreciate a world filled with people who believed in a different God—they would have to embrace them and love them instead of trying to change them, before the world became what it needed to be.

Jamaica blamed many of the world's problems on the church. It was the ethnocentrism of the church that led to the death of Central America and Africa. The missionaries went there with the notion that leading the heathens to Jesus would save the world. In the process they stripped them of their culture and identity. In her opinion, the church has stripped the world of dark skinned people of their true identity. They have manipulated black people into believing that being Christian and acting European is the same thing.

She talked about how the black church has been used to teach black people how to conform to the racist society they once hated. "It taught us that

long hair is better than kinky hair," she said. "We've been taught to call straight and wavy good hair. The consequence is to look down on brothers with locks and braids, and women who decide to grow their hair natural rather than put chemicals in it so they can look white. The church has tricked black people into believing that God has a preferred way of dress. A suit and a tie for men, and dresses below the knees for women. Black people have been stripped of all that is theirs, and the church has been used to enforce the views." Simon knew how Jamaica felt. He felt the same way.

She despised the black church for its judgmental people. Instead of loving gays and lesbians, the black preacher cries, "God made Adam and Eve, not Adam and Steve." She detested the fact that many gay ministers, choir members and pew dwellers hid in the closet out of fear that they would be rebuked if the truth were told about their sexuality. She didn't think it was fair for a person to love God and have to deal with their lifestyle being used as an example of what it takes to end up in Hell when deacons beat their wives and cheat on them, when people drove nice cars and refused to help those with no place to live, when the greed of the church was evil and distasteful in the eyes of God, yet the only thing that matters to these holy people was who was having sex, how often and with whom.

Jamaica was tired of the show. Week after week she had witnessed women dancing in the church who refused to speak to her after the service was over. She had hoped the church would be a good place to locate good friends. She needed a female support group. Instead she discovered that they couldn't get past the fact that she was a threat. All they could see were her curves and her smile,

and they knew their boyfriends and husbands would drool over her.

Jamaica couldn't help the way she looked. It was shameful that Christians judged a person's conduct based on what they saw. Jamaica loved sex, but she was no ho. She slept with men she loved. It took her time to give up the stuff. She liked showing her skin. She liked it not because she was advertising for her next one-night stand. She liked it because it made her feel good.

On many occasions the women of the church had told her that her dress was not appropriate. On one Sunday one of the older sisters brought her a long handkerchief to place over her legs. That was the last straw. She never stepped foot in another church. She considered it sexist, narrow-minded, cruel, and judgmental. If the men of the church had a problem remaining focused on the message because of her legs, that's a matter for them to pray on. Don't blame her because of the weakness of another man.

Besides, if its appropriate outside the church, why is it banned within it? Jamaica would say she thought God ruled the earth. If God sees all things and knows all things, why do the rules change when we step into a church? Shouldn't we seek to live a certain way all the time? Why all the emphasis on what we do on Sunday, with little regard for what happens the rest of the week?

She was also critical of an institution that was dominated by male leadership, yet had as its membership mostly women. Why are all the deacons men? Why aren't there any female pastors? How can a man help me understand how it feels to be a woman? She wasn't opposed to listening to a

man speak; she just felt it necessary to open the gates for women to share their side of the story.

Jamaica wanted to stand by her man. She wanted to believe in what he did. She couldn't pretend when it came to Simon. She didn't believe in what he did. She believed in the way he wanted to do it, but couldn't trust that his way of wanting to do it would ever prevail in the real world of mean black folks. She wouldn't be present on Sundays. She wouldn't take her seat near the front and wear a big hat, and long dress to satisfy the people. She would walk up in their with her legs showing, her back out, and her breasts standing up for the world to wave at. That would keep him in trouble. She couldn't change for them. She didn't see the need. She had to be herself.

The problem was with the people's definition of holiness. Jamaica argued that holiness seemed to always be concerned with something sexual. Be it homosexuality, premarital sex, infidelity, or pregnancy before marriage, it is the hot topic of the church. It mattered more to people to get at these sexual sins than to raise other sins. Holiness wasn't about loving people, or treating them the way they deserved to be treated. Holiness was about calling people out when they did wrong. It was about calling a sin a sin, while making the assumption that you're better than them.

She rejected the prosperity gospel of many black churches. She grieved the loss of the day when the church taught people how to be connected. The issue that people wanted to learn is how to use God to get rich. Forget lifting up others, they wanted their pie in the sky. She had seen her share of preachers standing before the people informing them they wouldn't make it unless they paid their tithes. People would pay their tithes

instead of paying their rent. The worst part is when they go to the church for help and are told they can't get any help. They can't get help because it's their lack of responsibility that got them in trouble.

Simon decided to call Jamaica before she left. Her flight departed at 2:30 p.m. It was after 11:00 a.m.

"Hey baby, I don't smoke, but I feel like I could use a cigarette." The sex the previous night was better than ever. At the end of it all they both just glared at the ceiling as if to say, what was that? Where did that come from?

"I'm with you on that one baby. I was hoping you would call. I'm going to miss you. I miss you already."

"Have I told you how much I love you today," Simon couldn't tell her enough.

"Yes, but tell me again."

"Your mystic shape and star-lit brightness, unchanged by time's tempest, rolls heavens before me when you touch my hand. Sought by kings are you; even my princely heart that breaks to tear for you, seeks to see your brighter eye." It had been a long time since Simon had written poetry.

"I love it when you do that. I love you too," she moaned as she changed positions in bed.

"Are you still in bed?"

"Yeah. Someone wouldn't let me sleep last night."

"Will you be able to rest over the weekend?"

"That's the good news. I don't have to be at work until Tuesday. It's too bad you can't go with me."

"I know. I was thinking the same thing."

"Are you ready for the meeting tonight."

"As ready as I can get. The only thing I know to do is show up, keep my mouth shut and smile," he tried to laugh as if it was a joke. It wasn't. That's all he could do.

"The good thing is you have options, Simon. They need you more than you need them. They don't realize what they have."

"Or maybe they do and that's why they want me out."

"You do realize that you have other options don't you? You can teach, write, you could even compete for my job if you wanted to. I'm warning you though. This sister ain't going down easy." Jamaica knew how to make him laugh. She was right. Simon worked as a reporter at a television station after graduating. He had the charisma needed for television. "You have a Ph.D. from Princeton, Simon. How many black folks can say that? Do you realize how marketable you are?"

"I know I have options. I just want to be sure I'm doing what God wants me to do. I'm afraid of making a decision that's outside the will of God. It's hard to explain."

"No, I understand. I might be a hot ass sinner, but I'm not trying to make a decision that is outside God's will. I may not go to church anymore, but I do believe, Simon. "

"I know. There's a part of me that wants to walk away. The other part won't let me go. When I see the children and the people who have been touched by the work I feel called to stay. The only thing I know to do is wait."

"I just hope that you can go on your terms. If you have to leave it would be nice if you could say thanks but no thanks. It's better when you can walk away with your dignity instead of being cast out with the garbage. You know what I mean, Simon."

"I'm with you on that. It has crossed my mind. I've been thinking about doing that before the meeting. I could just say to everyone thanks for coming out, but I've decided to leave. The problem I have with that is so many of the people want to fight on my behalf. Is it fair for me to rob them of the chance to speak on my behalf."

"That's all fine and good Simon, but they're not the ones who will have to take the heat. When it's over you're the one who will have to pick the pieces back together. Besides, niggers and onions make you cry. The same people who smile and support you today will stab you in the back tomorrow. We both know that's true. Their loyalty is from one Sunday to the next. Once you do or say anything to go against their expectations they will turn on you. You know that's true. You end up staying for people who love you today, but will hate you tomorrow."

"It sounds like I have a lot to think about. It's so confusing. Thanks for listening"

"Anytime, sugar. I love being the black holy folk expert. I've dealt with enough over the years to have a graduate degree in niggerology." They laughed again.

"Oh yeah, what are the core courses?"

"You didn't know? Let me school you, boyfriend. Backbiting 101, Dynamics of gossip, How to market a rumor, Techniques in eye rolling, How to judge an innocent Negro without guilt or shame. After all of that you write your thesis. Good examples have been, How to move up the ladder on others people's pain." They both hollered and rolled on the floor.

"Girl, you are a certified lunatic."

"That's why I get paid the big bucks. There's more here than a nice ass and pretty face. I know my black folks."

"When will I get to see that fine ass again?"

"Now the truth is out. All you want to see is my ass."

"Excuse me! Darling, love of my life, woman of my dreams, when will I see you again?"

"You've got my number. Call me. I'll be in New York in two weeks for the last interview. Can a brother say a prayer for a sister on that one?"

"You got it. It sounds like we're both in transition. Only God knows what will happen next."

•

"You ain't nothin' but a lie. Ya'll need to open your eyes. He ain't nothin' but a lying cheat," the words rung in Simon's ears like the sound of thunder in the peak of a storm. "I ain't comin back here until he's gone." She left the room. One of the preachers. One of the faithful followers. She walked out in the middle of the meeting. Before Simon had a chance to say I'm sorry. Before he had a chance to explain. She walked out. Frustrated, defeated, unwilling to bend.

Simon simply sat there. No words to defend himself were executed. The judge and the jury had spoken. The sentence was pending. He had traveled down this road enough to know that it didn't matter what he said. They didn't care. They, the other side, wanted him out at any cost. They would do whatever they could to get him out.

Simon had become numb to the old song and dance. Each month they gathered for business meetings at Shady Grove. Each month they gathered to decide on the business of the church. Each month they went through the attack. Simon

knew it was coming. All he could do was sit back and bear it. Bear the pain of rebuke. The pain of false accusations. Over time he had learned to say nothing. To numb himself to the attack.

"She's right! He ain't nothin' but a lie," another faithful leader added to the attack. A trustee who Simon had leaned on through the years for support and guidance. One who he considered a friend—lashed out at him. The attack thickened. When would it end? How many others had turned their backs on Simon? Still, he said nothing.

Thoughts, deep thoughts, circled through his mind. Thoughts of past accomplishments. Thoughts of sacrifices made for the ministry. Thoughts of people loved. People who he prayed for daily, who now circled the wagons preparing for the attack. Why me? What did I do? Is it as bad as it appears? Thoughts, deep thoughts, kept circling his mind as Simon built yet another wall around his heart to protect himself from the attack.

He thought of the growth of the ministry. In fourteen years they had increased membership at a phenomenal rate. More than 1,400 persons had united with the church. In fourteen years they had constructed a new building to accommodate the growth in membership. In fourteen years the church had moved from a small church hidden in the trees to a major player in the doings of the city.

"Brother Pastor, you need to get it together. We're tired of your games. We keep coming back to this place. Over and over again you tell us that things will get better, but here we go again," Deacon Andrews uttered. Fire snorting from his soul. The attack continued. One after another. Why me? What did I do? The thoughts circled his mind as the enemy continued to circle the wagons.

"Is it all worth this?" a thought hit. "Is it worth this? These no count, ungrateful niggers don't care about you. Is it worth the struggle." A part of Simon wanted to resign. The other part refused to give them that satisfaction. That's what they wanted — surrender. "Walk away and start your own ministry," another thought hit. "The people will follow you. They're just as tired as you are." That sounded good. He needed a new place. A place where he would receive appreciation for what he did.

Who am I? Could it be that they're right? Maybe I'm wrong. Who am I? What does it all mean? Where is it all headed? The struggle of being the Preacha' Man had caught up with Simon. The pain of dealing with black folks who cared little about the impact their words have on the preacher, had created a place in him — a place where he no longer knew who he was. Simon lost himself amidst the words, the attacks of the circling enemy. He had become too numb to speak.

Each month, the same song and dance. Each month the stress of potential pain. Who am I? Why do I do it? Is it worth the struggle? Why not walk away, start your own thing? Why not walk away from the work of ministry and live like real people? The Preacha' Man was lost. All that remained was a façade. The people received what they wanted. A veil of holiness covered the real Simon. All they saw was the Preacha' Man. A fake man. A lie. A messed up, confused bundle of pain.

"I'm sorry if I've hurt anyone," the Preacha' Man spoke. Was he really sorry? "Forgive me for the things I said, or done to create these feelings in your life." Did he mean that? Could he mean that? The Preacha' Man spoke. Simon said what he was supposed to say. He was supposed to be forgiving.

He was supposed to be holy, sanctified, filled with the Holy Spirit. Holy Man. Preacha' Man. That's what he's supposed to say. "If we can come together and pray for healing," that sounded good.

"No, I won't listen to this," they continued to circle the wagons. Another left. Another followed.

Simon thought the worse had come. Things then got worse. Deacon Andrews stood to speak. "Before all of you leave, we have someone who needs to speak," many who began to leave returned to their seats. "Sophie, the church Administrative Assistant has something to say."

Simon was surprised by this move. Sophie had informed him that she would not come to the meeting. He felt the worst coming. He knew she was still hurting because of his rejection. She walked to the front with her head bowed. She never looked at Simon.

"This is the hardest thing I've ever had to do," she started. "I'm doing it not because I want to, but because it's the right thing to do. There comes a time when certain things have to be exposed.

"I've worked in the office for a long time. I've seen and heard many things. Some of the things I let slip by. Part of my job is to protect the pastor. I protect him from people. I do my best to help him do his job. I've done that. The problem is now things are beginning to affect me.

"The rumors about the pastor are true. Women are coming from everywhere. Some of them come in from out of town to meet the pastor at fancy hotels. He met with one earlier this week. They come into his office and stay for a long time with the door closed. I've asked him to keep the door open because it doesn't look good. He never listened. He

said he was counseling them and he needed to protect their confidentiality.

"I accepted that. I did my best not to read too much into things. That's until the pastor came on to me. He asked me out. He told me he needed a person to help him with the pressure. He told me things were bad at home and he didn't know what to do."

Simon wanted to speak, but he kept quiet. How could he address Sophie's lie? Who would believe him? All he could do was trust that the people would not believe her.

"When I told him no, he wouldn't listen. He would stare at my breasts and legs and make comments about how good they looked. He would ask me about my personal life. He always wanted to know who I was dating. I told him that was personal. He said part of his job was to ensure that all my needs were being met.

"Only yesterday he lost his temper. He told me there were expectations that came with my job. He wouldn't tell me what they were, but I knew what he meant. I was scared I'd lose my job. That's why I'm here tonight. I think he took things too far."

The room was buzzing. Simon could tell that many of his supporters were influenced by Sophie's statement. "You have anything to say in your defense?" Deacon Andrews asked as he fought back the grin.

"All I can say is I'm sorry I hurt you Sophie. I'm sorry I hurt you so bad that you would have to resort to that. You know what I mean. You know that's not true," that was all he could say. He bowed his head. He wanted to pray. He was too hurt to try. The betrayal of the ministers was one thing, the lies told by others was another, the lie told by Sophie

hurt even more. He had cared for her. He hired her because she needed help. He protected her from termination when the wolves complained. Her job performance never met his expectations. Now she turned on him. He had loved her and supported her because she needed help.

Was her love for him so deep that she would resort to this? Was she hurt that bad? Simon reflected over the years he'd spent with her. It was shameful that it had come to this. What could he do? He did nothing.

"We have more to share," Deacon Andrews continued the witch-hunt. "The Bible tells us that those who rule over us need to be able to control their own household. We have a problem with the pastor's home. It's bad enough that he doesn't respect his wife enough to be faithful. His actions have led her down the wrong path." What was this about? "Sister Jackson, come forward."

Francine Jackson was one of Janet's friends. They served together with the youth ministry. She'd been to their house for dinner. She came forward in a daze.

"This for me is the hardest thing I've ever done," she started. "Janet and me have been friends since she came to Shady Grove. Our children go to school together. My husband and I have spent quality time with Janet and the pastor. I love them. I'm also concerned for them."

"A few months back Janet asked me to meet her for lunch. She was hysterical. At lunch she confided in me. She told me something that shocked me. I had looked up to her as a model for women. I trusted her to help me learn more about being a godly woman. That day she told me she was having

an affair. If that wasn't bad enough it's with one of the members."

"That's enough!" Simon stood. "It's one thing for you to crucify me. You can tell your lies and harm me, but keep my family out of this. They didn't sign up for this. If there are any issues involving my wife, that's between the two of us. We'll take care of that on our own. I don't need, no, we don't need this. This is inhumane!"

"You got one thing wrong," a woman shouted back from the back of the church. "It is about us. What the two of you do behind closed doors is about us. Like it or not, it is our business, and she did sign up for this when you said you wanted to lead us." A few claps could be heard in response.

"I don't know," Stan from the Bible study group stood to speak. "It sounds to me like you have a lot out there that is rumor. I would think that we'd want to investigate this mess before we put it out here. Anybody could make up stuff. With all that's going on to get rid of the pastor, I wouldn't be surprised if stuff has been made up."

"That ain't rumor!" the same woman shouted. "Everybody knows Janet's screwing Maurice Burt! Everybody knows he's a stripper" A silence hit the room. Apparently everyone knew but Simon. He felt like a bigger fool. Not only had his wife been having an affair, she had done it in view of everyone. He had been so busy dealing with his own pain that he didn't know what everyone knew. Had he been that self-absorbed? Had he been that big a fool? Did she go to him because of the sex? Was it because he wasn't good enough in bed?

"Even if that's true, that don't have nothing to do with the pastor. He didn't make her do that. He can't make her do right. If that's true, she's

responsible for her own actions, not him." There was some truth to his statement, but wasn't Simon partially to blame for what happened?

For the next four hours people pranced to the front of the church to give their spin on things. Many were passionate about the need for a change. Others talked about the difference Simon had made in their lives. They were willing to forgive, love and move forward. It was time for a vote. The process deadened Simon. It no longer mattered which way the vote went.

Robert Sargent, one of the trustees came forward to read the recommendation from the Board of Deacons and Trustees. "This task has fallen upon me. It is not one I choose, it is one that has been chosen for me," he pulled out a piece of paper from his pocket and read the recommendation. "The Joint Board of the Shady Grove Church recommend that Simon Edwards be terminated effective immediately as the Pastor of the Shady Grove Church."

"We need a motion to accept the recommendation," Deacon Andrews said.

"So moved," Simon heard the voice but did not look to see who spoke.

"I second the motion," another unknown critic cried. It no longer mattered what side they stood on. It all felt the same. It all felt like dry bones in the valley.

"Okay, we're ready to vote. I'm going to ask that we do this by standing. Any one have a problem with that?" No one said a word.

"Are you ready to move on the motion?" Time was getting close. This was the moment all had been waiting for.

"Move on the motion."

"All in favor of the motion which calls for the termination of the pastor please stand."

They stood. Simon anticipated the end. What he found confused him. For over four hours they fought on his termination. It seemed like the end had come. When the time came to vote only 45 people stood. 45 people. All of this noise for 45 people. His life put out for public view for 45 people. All of the 45 had spoken. They took their jabs. They fought their fight to the end.

"All opposed to the motion stand," it was like an earthquake. Too many to count. More than 200 on the other side. They stood proud. They were proud of their pastor. Their lives had been touched. They believed in him. They were not moved by the words, even Sophie's confession. They didn't care. They wanted to keep their pastor.

"Do you all know what you're voting on?" Deacon Andrews challenged with a tone of frustration.

"Yes!" they yelled in unison.

"The motion fails," Deacon Andrews put an end to the mess. The people clapped. Some cried. Some hugged each other. It was a time of celebration. It wasn't for Simon. He should have felt relief. Instead he was confused.

The people waited for a victory speech. Simon needed to say something to bring an end to the chaos. He didn't have anything to say. "Deacon Caldwell, would you please pray," He couldn't do it. Too much pain and he couldn't show it. "Let us hold hands. As we do that, I want to thank all of you for being here tonight. Thanks for your support. We have to move on"

As Deacon Caldwell prayed, Simon struggled. Memories flooded his soul. Memories of years gone by. Memories of sacrifices made.

Memories of lack. Memories of tears cried. Tears cried due to lack of money to pay the bills. Memories of a church that failed to offer a raise when it was justified. Memories of his children going without. Memories of a building built without consideration of his input. Memories of the words just uttered, "He's a lie. I won't come back until he's gone." The memories made him sad. He cried, but not on the outside.

The Preacha' Man remained strong. Be strong and courageous. Be strong and courageous. Be strong, be strong. The Preacha' Man within Simon begged to keep the tears inside. They wanted to come out. He wanted to scream, "Leave me alone. Leave me alone. Let me live. Love me, help me, hold me, stand with me. Please, please!" The man within begged the Preacha' Man — let me out. No, stay there. Don't let them see you.

Memories and tears. Memories and pain. Thoughts and frustration. The Preacha' Man took over. After the prayer Simon walked to his office. The people approached. He couldn't speak. He walked gingerly. "Hurry up," the Preacha' Man warned. Through the sanctuary he walked, slowly. He opened the door. Simon closed the door behind him clearing himself from the circling crowd. The tears came. First one, then two, then more and more. They came uncontrollably. He couldn't stop them now. He ran to his office hoping no one would see him.

There, in his office, the man came out. It felt good. The tears cleansed the part of Simon that needed healing. Alone, there in his office, he found religion again. The man came out granting the Preacha' Man a reprieve from the game of holiness. This was no time for games. The wall came down.

The pain came out. The tears flooded his soul and cleansed the dried up dungeon of despair called his life. The man came out. The Preacha' Man went away.

The Preacha' Man had to go away for Simon to find God. For God to find him, the Preacha' Man had to take a walk. God demanded his tears. God desired to wipe away the tears. The Preacha' Man wouldn't let God.

"God take my pain. God take my weaknesses. God take my loneliness. God take the stress of never being good enough. God take the agony of the rejection and the pain of under compensation. Give me the strength to know that you are in control of it all." Simon found himself. He prayed for himself. It was time, after all these years, for the real man to emerge.

What does one do after a night like that? What does it take to inspire and uplift after coming that close to the end? Simon saw his life flash before him, and he didn't like what he saw. He saw a man confused over the varied voices in his head. He saw a man hurting. He saw a preacher trying. He saw a man with a deep hole in his soul. He saw a faithful preacher willing to work to make a difference.

Back and forth he toddled. Back and forth between strength and weakness. He didn't sleep well that night. He remembered the night he almost relapsed. After the meeting he thought of getting high again. He had no one to turn to. No one to hold. The glare of the young drug dealer haunted him throughout the night. "Yo, what ya need?" The words of the young dealer would not let him rest. How did I end up there? How could I consider using again after all these years? How could he go on?

Simon had to move on, but he wanted to stand still. He was so numbed by the attack that moving was the last thing on his mind. He wanted to hear stillness. No more attacks. No more voices. His need was for silence and stillness. The reality of the moment required that he do something. It required that he do something soon.

It was then that he accepted what he had known deep down for a long time. He was tired of being the Preacha' Man. He didn't want it anymore. Simon wanted ministry, but he didn't want the stress of being what the mob demanded. He could never live up to their expectations. He would never have enough time or energy to be all that he needed to satisfy their desire.

Simon knew that he wanted to walk away. Not just from the work of Shady Grove, but from the work of organized religion. He couldn't take it. It was then that he realized that the church was like a drug. It felt good when injected. It felt good on Sunday morning. It felt good when lives were being changed and people said Amen. It felt good when they shouted and danced and clapped and prayed and praised and laughed. It felt good when injected. But the down side was the come down. After the preaching and praying; after the shouting and dancing came the let down. After Sunday morning there was the let down of the real world.

The attack was like a bad hangover. The church was like a drug—good when high, bad when not. It was then that he knew that he had to kick the habit. Simon had to let it go. He needed to walk away, yet needed the fix of Sunday morning.

How did Simon get to this place? The revelation of his addiction to the church had settled in. He was out of denial. He faced his demon and

hated what he saw. He saw a man dwindling day-by-day, moment-by-moment. He saw a lost self.

"Be strong," the Preacha' Man was still there. He wouldn't let Simon go. "Don't cry. Be strong."

•

Getting into bed was difficult. Even more difficult was looking Janet in the eye. He returned home from the attack with a list of questions for her. Was it his fault she had the affair? How did everyone else know while she kept the secret from him? How did she get involved with a stripper? Was he better in bed? It shouldn't mater, but for some strange reason it did. It mattered to Simon that his wife had sex with a known stripper and he didn't know. It mattered that everyone else knew. He felt like a fool. He felt used. He felt like less than a man.

"How was the meeting?" Janet asked as Simon walked into the bathroom to change clothes to go to bed.

"It was crazy," he said. "They voted. I can stay."

"That's great if that's what you want."

"I don't even know what I want anymore."

"I understand. It was that bad?"

"It was worse than that. Sophie turned against me. She told them I approached her about sex."

"So, she gave in."

"Gave in to what?"

"You didn't know."

"Know what Janet."

"The deacons and trustees raised $10,000 for Sophie to turn on you. You didn't know that?"

"No! How would I know?"

"Everyone else knew."

"That seems to be the rule of the night. There's a lot that everyone knew but me."

"What else?"

"Someone brought up your relationship with the stripper. They said it's the talk of the town. I guess no one thought to talk to me." Janet could tell that Simon was hurt.

"That's what happens when you talk to your friends. I guess I learned a lesson. You can't trust anyone in the church when it comes to your personal business. Other people can, but we can't. I'm sorry Simon. I didn't mean for that to happen."

Simon couldn't blame Janet for sharing her pain. He understood the need to share. He needed the same thing. His problem was there was no one to share his with. If he had found a person, their conversation could have been a subject for the meeting.

"Janet, I don't have anyone to trust. As I left the meeting I discovered I've never had that. My life has been devoid of friends since I entered the ministry. This life is lonely. I've always known that, but I never knew how lonely it is before tonight. I never knew how much of our life is open for public display and how critical they are of what they hear."

"I know," Janet agreed. "It's taken a toll on me too."

"How so?"

"The people never stop to think of how their attack on you impacts me and the children. We hear things. The kids hear people talking about you all the time. It happens when we go out to eat. It happens at the grocery store. We can be minding our own business and come across people talking about something you supposedly did. That hurts

us. It scars us too. They don't think about that. They never stop to think about our being human."

"That's sad."

"They don't think about why we have problems in our marriage. Part of it is because they won't keep their noses out of it. If we cry they know about it. If we mess up, they know. If they think we're close to messing up they know."

"It is worse than I thought," Simon was taking it all in. He hadn't thought about how Janet and the kids dealt with his life.

"It's the reason I don't hold you like I used to, Simon. Not because I love you less, but because I hate our life. I hate these people. I hate what they have done to us. I hate what they will do to our children. I can't take them any more."

"Is that why you had an affair?"

"It's for the same reason you had an affair, Simon. It's because you had needs that couldn't be met at home. It's because you found yourself at a place where you hurt too much and you couldn't take no more. It's because you got tired of living up to the expectations of people who didn't try to do the same in their own life. I did it because I need someone to help me get away from it all, and you were too caught up in how it messed with you to see I needed you. You couldn't help me and I couldn't help you because we needed something else."

"Why a stripper? Was it because he was better in bed than me?"

"So, they brought that up. To be honest, at first it was because of his body. The first time was because he looked good and he showed an interest in me. Do you know how long it's been since a man told me I'm sexy? That fine, dark skinned man told me I was the best looking woman in the room. After he told me that I was gone."

"I've told you the same thing."

"It's not the same. It's not the same because it was said out of habit. When you say it I don't feel the passion."

"Was he better than me. Is that why you kept doing it?"

"That's your ego talking. Why do you brothers go there? What do you want to know? Was his dick bigger? Yes. Was his body better? Yes. Was he better in bed? Not necessarily. When we used to make love there was a chemistry that I've never felt. I haven't felt that for a long time. I don't feel it because I don't feel that you love me anymore."

"That makes sense."

"I could ask you the same thing. Was Jamaica better in bed? Did she have a firmer ass and tits? Did she suck your dick better than me? I could ask you the same thing, but I don't have to Simon. I don't have to because I know the answer. I know because on the rare occasions when we make love I know you're wishing you were making love to her instead of me. I can see it in your eyes. I know that look."

Janet was right. There was no need to harp on the subject. He could tell she was beginning to get angry.

"I have made my mistakes. So, you think it would have been different if I went to law school?"

"It would have been different. I don't know if the outcome would have been different. I don't know if you would have stayed away from Jamaica if you were an attorney instead of a slave to the church. I do know it wouldn't have been as stressful."

It was time for Simon to come clean. "I was with Jamaica the past two nights. It's the first time I've seen her since the last time."

"I know."

"How did you know?"

"I saw her at the mall yesterday. I knew it had to be her. She looked good."

"All the other rumors are lies Janet. I never slept with Bonita. I wanted to, but I never did."

"I know."

"How do you know?"

"Because if that old-ass heifer ever got hold of your fine ass she'd never let you get away," she smiled and laughed.

"I needed that."

"I mean it Simon. You were the best. No, you are the best."

Simon looked at his wife. He looked in a way that had been missing. He saw what had been lost. He kissed her. It was a different kind of kiss. The kiss said thank you for loving me. Thank you for supporting me. Forgive me for dragging you into this mess.

"Janet, You're so sexy. I want to make love to you."

"I thought you'd never ask."

They made love like old times. It was better than that. They made love like it was the first time. The love returned for a night. They needed each other after being the subject of a public trial. No one else would understand. It was the seal on a life of ups and downs. They did love each other. Love wasn't enough. It was enough for the night. That's all that mattered.

Chapter Six - Friday

"And he said, it is finished"

THE ANSWER TO THE PRESENT IS OFTEN FOUND IN THE PAST. For years Simon had hidden from the demons of his past. Without knowing it these demons had stripped him of his humanity. All that remained was a mere figment of what could be. The Preacher stood before the people pretending to be content with life. The man stood isolated from the people, and unaware of what it meant to be a man.

Way back in the past was the key to all the dismay. The tears were locked away in the past. Simon couldn't cry before things fell apart. He couldn't cry because all the pain had been numbed by the pretension. Who am I? What am I? Where am I going? These questions could never be answered without going back-way, way back to days when life hurt more than the attack.

The attack reminded Simon of what he worked to overcome. So much to overcome, and so little to work with to achieve his goal of wholeness. The confusion left him wondering, "Who am I trying to convince? Am I the Preacher for me, or for them?

Could it be that I'm doing it all to convince myself that I'm okay? I'm okay with God." Simon needed to know that he was okay with God, yet the more he tried the more it felt like God had closed the windows of heaven, preventing the blessing from flowing his way.

The answers were found way, way back in the past. The day after the attack Simon discovered a man who had failed to deal with the pain. The pain had now resurfaced to pull him deeper into an abyss. That night, it felt like he would never escape the pain. The more he cried, the more he hurt.

It hurt that the church had turned it's back on him. His spirit was weary. Deep down he knew the worse had not yet come. More was in store. More pain. More rejection. More would come because of what he knew. Things would have to change. If he didn't change his circumstances, he would lose the last piece of life left. He had to go back. He had to face the past.

Facing the past taught him an important lesson. Part of the problem was himself. What happened to him that night wasn't simply caused by mean people who searched for weak preachers to stab in the back. It happened to him, in part, because of what he had created. He had become cold and unmoving. The people noticed that his work in ministry was habitual. He did the work void of passion.

The past had ruined his present. He had to go back into his secret closets to do some serious spring-cleaning.

•

Simon was walking home from school. It was springtime, his favorite season. Dandelions and clovers painted the grass. The sun was bright, and

the birds were chirping. It was springtime. He was happy.

As Simon approached Banks Avenue he noticed the clouds. Simon loved the clouds. If he were to look long enough he could find figures in the sky. His mother told him it was God's way of reminding people of God's presence. God looks down on us from heaven, and if we look hard enough, we can find God in the clouds.

Simon looked. He looked some more. Up in the sky he found a figure that looked like Jesus. His parents had a picture of Jesus in their bedroom. He's kneeling in that picture. His eyes are looking up, and there's a ray of light that breaks through the clouds. Simon loved that picture.

That picture taught him what Jesus looked like. Long blonde hair, blue eyes, and a beard. Simon could see him in the clouds. "There's his eyes, there's his nose, there's his beard," he whispered as he crossed the street. "Jesus loves me, this I know. For the Bible tells me so," he sang.

It was his favorite song. His mother would sing it sometimes. She cried when she sang, but Simon knew they were good tears. He always felt better after his mother sang.

"Nigga get out of my way," three older white boys yelled at him. He was taken by surprise. He hadn't seen them coming. He was so busy looking at the Jesus in the sky that he hadn't seen or heard them coming.

"I said, get out of my way," another boy uttered. Simon did his best to get out of the way, but it was too late. The one with blond hair grabbed his arm. The one with black hair kicked him in the side. The other slammed Simon into an oak tree.

They beat him, and beat him, and beat him some more.

"That'll teach you nigga," the biggest kid said as he spit in his face.

"What did I do?" Simon cried.

"Next time walk on the other side of the street when you see us comin'," they laughed. They left Simon there bloodied and crying. "What did I do? Why me? Why did they call me nigga?" Simon cried some more.

He gazed at the sky in search of answers. The Jesus in the sky had faded away. With him, faded Simon's dreams. It was his first encounter of racism. He understood why Daddy drank, and why Mother wept. He knew why the older black boys didn't try. From that day on, the world looked different. He no longer noticed the figures in the sky, and the flowers that painted the grass. He no longer sang, "Yes, Jesus loves me." He didn't believe that anymore. It was the day the sun died.

Simon wanted to get even, but didn't know how. All he could do was get up and run home with his bruised pride.

Every black kid has a memory like that. Sadly, racism can rob one of their dreams. Simon was too young to deal with racism. It was a time to enjoy life. He should have been playing in the grass, not using it to soak the blood from his beaten body. He was too young to understand why this was happening. He still didn't understand.

That day became a defining moment. He vowed to never let a white boy beat him again. Never again would he be caught off guard. Never again would he trust the blue-eyed Jesus that hung on the wall. That Jesus didn't look like him. That Jesus looked like the boys who called him a nigger and threw him into a tree and beat him on the

ground. That Jesus didn't come to his rescue when he sang the song, "Jesus loves me this I know." Simon didn't know that Jesus anymore. If Jesus loved him, why did this happen? What did he do to deserve this? Without knowing it, Simon's faith in God was dwindling.

•

It was the year Frazier beat Ali. It was the year Simon met God for the first time. He met God at the Mt. Celestial Baptist Church. Every Sunday, Simon and the other children in his neighborhood would wait for the church bus to pick them up for the long trip to God's country.

Simon could care less about singing in the choir, but it was the in thing to do. All the boys were in the choir and his failure to do so would have made him look bad. He joined church without understanding what it all meant. The next thing he knew the preacher was talking about baptism. "What's baptism?" he asked on the way back home.

"They throw you into the water," Darron, one of his friends, answered. Simon was ready to change his mind. The last thing he needed was to be thrown into water. He almost drowned a few months prior after jumping into the deep end of the pool without knowing how to swim. Someone told him the best way to learn to swim was to jump in, and like a fool, he believed them. He wasn't about to get suckered again.

"What you mean they throw you in the water?" he responded with terror on his face.

"It ain't no big deal man. They just dump you. It's like takin a bath," Gerod said, easing his mind for a moment. Taking a bath was something he could handle. Being thrown into the pool was something he would never do again.

Simon was allowed to sing in the choir immediately. Rehearsals were held at the pastor's house a few blocks away from his neighborhood. Once a week the gang walked to Reverend Butler's house. There, in his living room, his wife would lead the rehearsal. She meant well, but lacked skills. She had to be at least 80.

Despite her age and lack of talent, they gladly walked to her house each week to practice old hymns. It was a choir of young people from the 'hood — six guys and seven girls. For many of them it was the highlight of the week.

Reverend Butler was a kind soul. He cared for the youth, and they knew it. They all gravitated to him. Simon listened to every word. He watched him walk. He was God on earth to Simon. He loved him. He wanted to be like him.

It was there, in his living room, that Simon said his first public prayer. It was after choir rehearsal that Butler asked, "Would one of you like to lead us in prayer?"

"I would," Simon said. He prayed with ease. It felt natural. He knew then that this was for him. Back then, in the 6th grade, He knew that ministry was his calling. After praying he felt something warm on the inside, something special. He prayed for the hungry children. He prayed for God to bless them in their singing. Everyone said Amen. They walked home as usual. No one mentioned his prayer, but it was the only thing on his mind.

Simon couldn't wait for the following Sunday. He made comments in Sunday school like never before. The Bible meant something to him. He enjoyed talking about Jesus. His teachings were both inspirational and practical. For the first time in a long time he felt the words of Christ. Not since

that day when the figure of Christ faded from the sky had he felt like singing about Jesus.

They sang that Sunday. All the boys wore maroon shirts with gray pants. Simon's pants were lighter than the others, but he didn't care. He enjoyed singing, and the people enjoyed their singing. He didn't care how he looked. He didn't even care how he sounded. Simon simply wanted to be like Reverend Butler, one used by God to make a difference.

Three weeks later Simon was baptized. Three others were baptized with Simon. It was a big deal; at least it was for everyone else. The truth is he didn't understand the fuss. Sure, he enjoyed the teachings of Jesus, and wanted to be like Reverend Butler, but this dumping ceremony didn't make much sense to Simon.

Simon did it because he wanted to sing in the choir. He figured it was a worthwhile sacrifice. He stepped into the water. The Holy Man looked at him and said, "I baptize you in the name of the Father, the Son, and the Holy Spirit." He then took Simon down for a bath. The water was cold.

The people were happy when he came out. His mother was happy. His father was happy. Some woman was shouting; she was happy too. They rushed Simon to the bathroom where he changed clothes. It was over. He was officially a Christian.

The events of the next few months shattered Simon's world. Reverend Butler became ill. He was an old man. Six months later he died. It was the first time Simon confronted death. Death was something he read about, but never had to deal with face to face. No one told him about the grieving process.

The holy man's death rocked Simon's world. It came during a time when the pieces were coming together. He was healing from being stripped of his youthfulness in the truck. The pain of Iowa had begun to subside. The question of race, and the torment of having been thrown into a tree, kicked and called nigger, was a distant memory. Then, the holy man died.

His death took a part of Simon that began to believe again. Who could he trust now? Even God had failed him. How could Simon be like the holy man without him near to show the way? There was no need to cling to that vision. Simon couldn't be like him now. The doors of Heaven, once again, had locked him out.

It was the first funeral Simon ever attended. He sat in the back. He cried bitterly. He sat there, cried, and prayed the prayer of rage. "Why you do this to me God?" He demanded an answer. He wanted to know why God would bring this wonderful man into his life and then take him when he needed him the most.

"If you love me, why?" Didn't God know he needed a guide? His life had been turned upside down, and this man had reached him like no one before. His confidence was high. He had a goal, and it was a good one. "Why God? Why?"

In the back of the church, Simon sat—alone. He sat begging for answers. He waited for the heavens to open and for a voice to answer his question. It never happened. The longer he sat, the madder he became. He was mad at God. He was mad at Reverend Butler, but more than anything, he was mad at the church.

He was mad at the church for lying to him. They promised God would take care of things. Some would shout, "He may not come when you

want, but he's always on time." That's a lie, he thought. He didn't come on time. He begged for an answer he never received. Simon was told that Jesus stands at the door and knocks. They told him that if he opened the door Jesus would come in. He opened the door, but no one came in. All he felt was misery — no comfort, no peace, no joy.

Simon had been sold a bad bag of goods. There, in the back of the church, he vowed never to go back to church. It hurt too much to go back. He was tired of the broken promises. Again someone he trusted turned their back on him. Someone he needed left him to deal with the pain alone.

No one comforted Simon. No one said, "Everything will be alright." Arms were wrapped around his widow. She cried too. Other members of the family were there — they received comfort — but Simon, he was left in the back of the church to wipe away his own tears. Each teardrop exposed a broken promise.

•

Simon knew things were bad for Crystal, but he never expected it to be so bad. They brought her home from the hospital after weeks of surgery and treatment. Simon was told the worse was still ahead.

Crystal's long beautiful hair was gone. So was her energy. She had lost the use of the right side of her body. The doctors said the tumor was the size of an egg. It was retrieved from her brain. They knew it was only a matter of time. Crystal would die. She was given six months to one year.

You never know how much you love someone until you're forced to deal with losing them. Crystal and Simon had a unique relationship. She was his younger sister. Younger sisters look up to their brothers. They look to brothers for

Preacha' Man

protection and comfort. That was the unspoken rule. If someone messes with your sister, you kick their ass. Crystal knew Simon had her back if things got out of control.

Everyone liked her. The news of her illness spread like wildfire. Her friends wanted to see her, but she needed rest. Her body was weak from the treatment.

Simon did his best to stay out of her way. He didn't know what to say or do. Brothers are supposed to be able to help—he couldn't. He couldn't stand to watch her suffer. "Why her, Lord?" he prayed. "Why not me?" He deserved the sickness. She attended church. She prayed faithfully. He was the pagan of the household. He deserved to die. She deserved to live.

Watching her suffer tore at Simon's soul. He needed to see her laugh and play. "Prove to me God that you can heal. If you are real, do something, and do it now." His anger toward God worsened with each passing day. Such a cruel punishment for an innocent person.

Maybe God was mad at him for not going back to church. Could that be the reason for her illness? Simon needed answers, but none came. All that followed was more confusion. He watched her suffer. He tried to be positive. The best way for him to do that was to stay out of her way. All he wanted to do was cry.

She never complained. She continued to pray. His mother would take her to church when she was up to it. There was a new church, the Progressive Missionary Baptist Church. The pastor was Harold Butler. Another pastor named Butler. Simon couldn't handle the pressure.

Services were held in an old storefront not far from where they lived. His mother and Crystal

158

would go to church. Daddy and Simon stayed home and listen to the blues and James Cleveland. Simon understood his father now. Music healed a lot of pain. Drugs helped even more. He couldn't make it through a day without drugs and music. Nothing else helped. Praying had been futile in the past, and besides, God apparently didn't care about Simon. All Simon had was drugs and George Clinton. His father had vodka and the blues.

It was the age of Funk. The P-Funk changed the canvass of the music industry. Parliament, Bootsy's Rubber Band, Funkadelics and a joint. That's what Simon's life had been reduced to—funk and drugs.

Sadly, he fell deeper and deeper without anyone noticing. Simon's older cousins taught him about the world of drugs. They taught him how to cop drugs, that is where and how to buy them. If he didn't have money he would hang with someone who had drugs or the money to buy drugs. He'd get high in the morning before going to school. He would leave school property during lunch to get high, and he'd fire one up after school.

Soon the marijuana wasn't enough to cover the pain. Simon graduated to acid and speed. He enjoyed the trip because it helped him forget Crystal's pain. That high soon wore thin, so he moved to riskier drugs—cocaine and heroin. Without realizing it Simon had evolved into a stone junky. No one knew. He covered his addiction behind Crystal's illness. Everyone was so busy worrying about her, that no time was committed to him. It was a nice set up. He could do what he pleased because no one had time to deal with him.

Simon needed help, and soon, but none was near. He quit the football team using as an excuse

the need for him to spend more time at home with his sister. The truth was he was too high to play. He floated in and out of school on a cloud. He could barely walk. Running was too much for him to handle.

He needed his parents to notice him. They were too busy with Crystal to notice. He drank and drugged because he felt no one cared. His life was empty. He wanted to die. Over and over again he begged God to take Crystal's illness and give it to him. He couldn't stand living anymore. He was the invisible man. No one noticed his pain.

Simon loved the way she smiled. He wondered if she knew. How could she know and walk with such confidence? She never complained.

"Run Simon," a voice yelled from the stands. Who could that be? Simon looked to his right, and there in the stands was Crystal. She was there with her cane. She was there with her wig covering her baldness. She had made the long walk of over a mile, as sick as she was, to watch him run.

No one had ever loved him like that. She cared enough to sacrifice her own health. He overheard her say, "That's my brother. He's gonna be good. You wait and see." He wasn't great, but she could see what Simon couldn't. He had what it took. She knew that.

Simon couldn't believe she was there. He wanted to cry. He wanted to hug her and tell her how much he loved her. What a girl! What a wonderful girl.

Simon ran like never before. He ran for Crystal and her love. He ran because she believed. He ran because she cared. He ran and won for the first time in his life. It wouldn't be the last win. He would win many races and break many records. That day she taught him about love and sacrifice.

•

The summer before her death, the family decided to send Crystal to Disneyland. Crystal had always wanted to go, so the family raised the money to send her. They all knew it was the last dance, but she didn't need to know.

It was then that Simon got his first whiff of journalism. The local newspaper, the Columbia Daily Tribune, learned of the trip. It was a good story, so they sent a reporter to their house to interview Crystal and her mother before the trip.

It was a good interview, at least it seemed that way. Simon's mother was excited about the trip. It would give her a chance to see her sister who lived in Santa Monica. Crystal was excited. She was a bit scared about the flight, but her desire to tug at Mickey's nose motivated her to get on that plane. They all laughed.

Simon remembered his mother pulling the reporter to the side. "She doesn't know she's dying. Please, don't put that in the paper," she said.

"Okay, Mrs. Andrews," he promised. They were both naïve to the workings of a newsroom. Simon didn't think much about Momma's request. Crystal would want to read the article—who wouldn't. If she didn't know about the seriousness of her illness, the last place you would want her to find out about it is in the paper.

The thing no one considered was her illness and anticipated death was the story. Readers would want to know that she was expected to die. It was a human-interest story. The reporter should have told them that.

It's the body bag approach to journalism. Give the reader or viewer all the details. Stick the microphone in the face of a grieving mother and take pictures of her crying. Get some good sound

bites of her sobbing. The audience loves pain. Forget that members of the family have to witness that.

The article appeared on the front page of the Sunday paper. It was a good picture of Crystal. They talked about her sense of humor, and her dream of going to Disneyland. Near the end he told the rest of the story. They shared that she was expected to die soon.

Crystal returned a bundle of joy. The trip did her good. Simon was still fuming that the family hadn't considered that maybe he needed to spend time with Crystal too. Disneyland would have been good for him. He understood that there was only enough money for two, but he wished he could have gone too, no one ever thought about that.

The night of her return was stressful. Mom cut out the picture from the paper for Crystal to see. They hoped she wouldn't see the article. It was too much to ask.

That night Simon heard her sobbing. In her room, next to his she cried through the night. She did it so no one else would hear, but she cried. Simon couldn't blame her. He would have cried before then. He had. His tears were enough to load a ship. They were enough for both of them, but she had not cried, at least Simon had not seen her cry.

That night he hated the newspaper. He wanted to write a nasty letter, but printing it would only add to the pain. He wanted to cuss them like a sailor, but he was too young for them to respect. There wasn't much that Simon could do other than to listen to his 13-year-old, dying sister cry.

•

They all gathered in the living room for the last breath. That's where Crystal had laid, in a coma, for the past four months. It was only a matter

of time. Simon's prayers had not been answered. The joy of the previous year was shattered by deep sleep.

Simon stood over her bed watching her breathe. Inhaling didn't come easy. Exhaling was easier yet appeared to be as painful. Inhale, exhale, it was only a matter of time. Why did it come to this? So much had happened in such a short space of time.

Standing there Simon remembered playing under the Christmas tree, playing in the back yard, singing and dancing to Diana Ross and the Supremes, playing the old man and woman from the hit television show *Laugh-In*. She would sit on the couch. He'd creep up next to her and say, "Can I have a little kissy wissy?" She would bop Simon on the head with her purse. Those were fun times. How did it come to this?

Simon remembered that day at the track, and the time she took his art portfolio to school for show and tell. Her classmates told Simon how proud she was. Now it came to this. He stared at her hoping for a miracle. Inhale, exhale.

Simon heard a voice, "Make me proud Simon," she said from her coma. He heard her speak to him. No lips parted. "Make me proud Simon."

Simon took a seat and held his head in his hands. He hurt too much to cry. He was tired of crying. He was too mad to feel.

"She's dead," his mother said. Silence.

Simon felt something inside. It was like a volcano ready to erupt. It was the sting of death boiling in his gut. He ran to his bedroom for the explosion.

"No, no, no, no, no, why, why why?!" It wouldn't stop. It couldn't stop. "Why you do this to me God? Why you hate me so much? I hate you!" The tears came when he thought he had no more to give. His sheets were wet with pain. He had nothing else to live for. No one to believe in him. All was lost—he thought.

He cried all the way to the funeral. The funeral made him cry more. Funerals are intended to help one heal from the pain. Sadly, the opposite is true. The hardest part was the funeral. What makes it hard is the crazy things people say that are intended to make you feel better.

"She's in a better place. It's the will of God. God never makes a mistake. Don't cry, God will take care of you," were some of the crazy things said by people who claimed to care. Simon wished they would shut their mouths. "I understand how you feel," some said. He knew that was a lie, because if they knew they would get out of his face.

No one knew how Simon felt. He was mad at God, and their words only made matters worse. If God never made mistakes, then why did God decide to take Crystal from him? Certainly that was a mistake given all the mess Simon was left to deal with on his own. If she was in a better place, why wasn't Simon with her? Simon agreed that it was Hell on earth, but why did she have to leave him here to deal with the Hell alone?

If it was the will of God, Simon didn't want anything to do with that God. That God was mean and vindictive. People of faith operate with some bad theology. Some of it comes from our pulpits. Preachers pass on views of God that limit people. They are left with more questions than answers.

If God is love, then why did he take a 13-year-old girl who has done no harm? Why do all the

bad people prosper, while the weak get weaker? Why talk about a God who passes out benefits upon death, while we grapple with life day after day? Simon had serious questions that weren't answered at the funeral.

He left depressed and confused. The eulogy said nothing. He couldn't remember who spoke or what was said. There were no answers, only questions. He left believing God had no time for him. After being raped, beaten, and denied, the only thing left was to get lost. It was time to hide, and that's what he did. He hid behind the clouds of drugs.

As Simon's parents dealt with grief in their own way, he dealt with his the only way he knew — drugs. He began using them more. He couldn't pray. If he could he didn't want to. All he wanted was to get high, and that's what he did.

To satisfy his growing habit Simon started selling drugs. A little marijuana. By the middle of his senior year in High School he had learned the craft well. He teamed up with a group of white boys and together they sold acid and cocaine to the rich kids. It was safe, at least it seemed that way. By dealing to the rich kids Simon protected himself from the police. Their focus was on the Douglas Park community, a.k.a., the 'hood. The police, media and adults were convinced that the drug problem was a black youth issue. Simon knew better. The real problem was with the young white kids who rebelled against their parents.

He sold the hard stuff. His closest friends never knew. He'd ride with them, get high, pick up girls, party, throw up, and go home. His parents were hurting too much to notice what had happened to their son. He went about business as usual — to

school in the morning, track practice in the afternoon, and high by sun down.

It was Simon's senior year in high school. Weeks had passed since he'd been to school. He didn't care anymore. Two suicide attempts had failed. Not once, but twice his stomach was pumped in the emergency room of the Boone County Hospital. His mother thought it was over a girl, Tammy, who broke up with him after getting pregnant by another boy, but that wasn't the cause. He wanted to die. He had no reason to go on.

After weeks in the psychological ward of the hospital, Simon was released. They found no reason to keep him. They knew he was depressed, but no one knew how low he was. He wanted to die. Simon was 17 years old with no future. Nothing, and no one to believe in. His parents didn't have time for him. His father was hurting, his mother was running, his sister was away, and the other sister was dead.

Simon had dropped out of school. His parents didn't know, but Mr. Battle, a counselor at the school knew. Mr. Battle was a legend in Columbia. A black man respected by whites and blacks alike. His wife was also an educator, and together they had touched the lives of countless children. Mr. Battle cared, and Simon didn't even know it.

Simon was home getting high. It was in the middle of the day. He was listening to some P-Funk when he heard a knock at the door. The knock got louder. He went to the door. "Who is it?" he asked bewildered.

"It's me, Simon. Mr. Battle. Let me in," he responded. Simon was surprised by his visit. He was happy to see him. He needed to be rescued, but

no one had taken the time to check on him. He needed to know someone cared.

Simon opened the door. "You come with me young man. You have been away from school long enough," he scolded. It felt good. Simon knew he had done wrong, but he didn't want to. He wanted to do the right thing, but the hurt was too deep, and he lacked support. Mr. Battle took Simon by the arm, led him to his car and drove him to school.

What he did next was revolutionary. "I understand you're a good writer," he said.

"I suppose so," Simon answered.

"This has been a tough time for you. We all know that, but you have to pull it together. I'm changing your schedule. I see you took American Literature with Mrs. Westerhoff and Brodie last year," he said. The class was a college prep course for gifted students. It combined history and literature over a two-hour period. Simon enjoyed the class, but more than the class, he loved the teachers.

"Yes, I did," he answered.

"Well, I'm changing your schedule. You will be working with Mrs. Brodie and Westerhoff as a student teacher. I want you to support them in whatever they need. I want you to spend an hour everyday writing. You need to get your feelings out. I'm told you have a future as a writer," he continued. Simon was surprised by his words. Where did he hear that? How did he know?

"I have a friend at the University of Missouri. His name is Thomas McAfee. He was a personal friend of James Baldwin. I want you to meet him. I want you to share your writing with him. It will be good for you," he said. For the first time in a long time Simon felt good inside. This man believed in

him. He was willing to do whatever it took to ensure he graduated.

Battle was not alone. There were other teachers who cared. Westerhoff and Brodie cared. There was another, a sociology teacher, who cared. One day Simon was depressed. She handed the class an exam. Simon couldn't concentrate. He wanted to cry. He wanted to get high. He signed his name, gave her his test and left the room. He ran to the bathroom where he spent the rest of the hour in tears. He didn't know why. He couldn't stop the tears.

Simon felt like a fool. Why couldn't he just suck it up and go on. By now he was trying to break the habit, but the drugs had gotten a hold of him. He wanted to make Mr. Battle proud, but something wouldn't let him go.

The next day the teacher asked Simon to stay after class. She closed the door, locked it, and sat in front of him. She was an older white woman like Westerhoff and Brodie.

"You want to fail, don't you?" she asked. Simon could feel a lecture coming. Did he want to fail? Maybe that was the problem.

"I'm not going to let you fail," she continued. She handed Simon the test from the previous day. There was an A in bold red letters on the top of the page. Simon didn't understand.

"My husband died of cancer last year. I know how painful it can be dealing with the loss of a loved one. I refuse to let you fail. You have too much to offer. I'm here for you. I care. I believe in you."

This white woman was telling Simon she cared. They were all around him. Coach Fred, the track coach, made Simon Co-Captain. He cared. He cared enough to let Simon stay with him when things got out of control at home. When his mother

threw him out, he was there. His teachers cared. The problem was Simon didn't care.

Simon graduated and was accepted to the University of Missouri. He didn't want to go, but he did. He started classes the summer after graduation. He was so lost. Simon didn't celebrate graduation. He felt he had nothing worth celebrating. No senior prom. No senior pictures. No class ring. No senior party—nothing. Simon walked across the stage, grabbed his diploma, and sobbed the night away. What would he do next?

College life was a bore. The summer courses weren't a challenge. Simon knew he could do the work, but he didn't want it. He enrolled because he didn't know what to do next. He had wanted to run track in college, but the school he wanted to attend, Westminster in Fulton, Missouri denied him admission because they said he couldn't afford to go. They had no track scholarships. Simon knew he could compete at the college level. He was a late bloomer. If given a chance he could make it, but he had wasted too much time. He didn't know what to do.

The summer session was a breeze, but the drugs were winning the battle. Simon had to do something, and quick. He went into his father's bedroom, found some money, and ran to the bus station.

"How far can I get with $22.50," he asked the cashier.

"You can go a lot of places. Where you want to go?" she responded.

"Give me a minute," he looked over the bus schedule. There it was. Warrensburg, Missouri. Simon had run well in Warrensburg. He was in a zone that night. "Give me a ticket to Warrensburg."

Simon took his ticket, jumped on the bus with no bags and headed to end the misery. He needed to get away from the drugs. He felt escape was the only answer. He left with no money, no clothes, no food. He had nothing.

Two weeks later Simon was homeless in a strange land. He knew no one. He had nothing to eat. At nights he broke into a Catholic Church close to the campus to sleep. His only nourishment was a bottle of orange juice that he had rationed for close to a week.

He couldn't take much more. It was time for a change. Either death or deliverance. Simon then did something that he hadn't done since Reverend Butler died. He prayed.

"I've tried this before God, and it didn't work. I know I've screwed things up, but I need help. I can't take no more." Simon felt God's peace. It took him by surprise. He felt loved by God. There, underneath an old oak tree, Simon heard, "It will be alright."

"Young man, can I help you?" It was a white man in a blue car. "You, under the tree, can I help you?"

He didn't know what to say. He was so weak. He had so many needs. He stood and walked to the car. "Aren't you Simon Edwards? You ran at Hickman High School. I'm Coach Pinkerton, the track coach here at Central Missouri State. Hop in." He was an angel. God had answered Simon's prayer.

•

Simon didn't realize it was a miracle. The blessing of that day didn't settle in until years later. If it had, things would have been different for him at Central Missouri State. God had provided Simon a second chance. Yes, he had prayed, but it didn't

sink in that what happened that day was God's answer to his prayer.

Things started out great. Simon stayed with Coach for a few days, and then moved into a dorm. Coach was a good man. Simon didn't know then that he was a strong man of faith.

It was time for the State Fair, and coach took Simon with him to work at the fair. He needed some cash to help pay for things the next semester. Coach took Simon, and a few other runners, with him to the fair. They worked in a variety of positions.

It was there, at the state fair, that Simon ran into his aunt. "Simon, is that you?" She ran up to him and hugged him. "Your mother is worried about you."

It had been months since Simon left Columbia. He had not called his parents. They didn't know what was going on. He wanted to call that day when he was under the oak tree, but didn't have a dime. He knew they were worried, but needed to focus on his own pain.

"Tell them I'm okay," he said.

"Where you been?" she asked.

"I'm in Warrensburg. I'll be running track at Central Missouri State. I'm here with the track coach." You could sense her relief. Simon was proud to tell her how he was doing. "Tell Mamma and Daddy not to worry. I'll be home as soon as I get things in order."

There was some order to his life. For the entire summer he stayed away from drugs. He had no choice. If there was a drug in Warrensburg, he didn't know how to find it. He enjoyed that summer. He talked to Coach about his future. He

shared some of his story. The coach listened. He cared.

The trimester started shortly after the State Fair. Before Simon knew it, Coach had the team preparing for the season. They were up early in the morning, lifted weights in the middle of the day, and worked out in the afternoon. By the end of the day, Simon was worn out. There was no time to rest. He had to study.

Simon was doing fine until he ran into the wrong crowd. This was his test. By the middle of the first trimester he was forced to deal with his two weaknesses—drugs and girls. The girls came first. They came from everywhere. It was hard for Simon to resist, and he didn't. After a while he wasn't sure who was using who—he them, or them he. They liked Simon because he was an athlete.

It didn't take long for Simon to develop a reputation as a dog. The girls were angry with him, and he understood why. He was looking for a good time, they were looking for commitment. He was too young to commit, but not too young to play. They should have known better.

The girls weren't Simon's biggest problem. Drugs were. He ran to Warrensburg to get away from drugs, but they found him. A few of his old high school chums enrolled at Central Missouri State. They knew Simon liked to get high, and they didn't want to get high alone. By the middle of the first trimester Simon was smoking weed again.

The worst of Simon's problems was a crazy white boy. They hung out together, smoked weed, did some acid and cocaine, chased women at the bars, and talked trash. He was into heavy metal, Simon was into P-Funk. When they were high, it didn't matter. When high, Pink Floyd sounded like Bootsy.

He was a white boy with a serious attitude. He was headed to prison, and fast. Simon did his best to stay away, but he had a way of finding Simon when he didn't want to be bothered.

There was a knock at Simon's door, "Stick, let me in," the crazy white boy shouted. Stick was Simon's nickname. It was 2:00 a.m. "Denise wants to see you man. She wants you bad."

"Who's Denise? Man go home," Simon shouted back.

"I ain't goin' back out there unless you come with me man. She said either you come out, or she's comin' up." Simon's roommates were angry. It was bad enough that they had three roommates in one room, having a nut knock on your door at 2:00 a.m. will put a serious damper on your sleep.

Simon walked downstairs with him. "Who's Denise man?" He demanded an answer. "What the fuck she want? It better be good." He was angry.

"It is good man. It's real good," he chuckled. Simon knew then that he was on something strong. He was afraid of what might come next.

Once outside they walked toward a storefront around the corner from the dorm. "Come over here man. You stand here while I get the shit."

"What the Hell ya talkin about?" Before Simon could say another word two police cars pulled up. Their lights were flashing. They jumped out. Simon slowly walked away. His natural instinct would have been to run. He walked. He was tired, shocked, and mad, but he walked.

They pulled the crazy white boy out from inside the music store. Glass was everywhere. Apparently he had thrown a brick into the glass window before coming to get Simon. One of the

neighbors had witnessed what he did and called the police. They were close by waiting for his return.

"Hey, Stick! Tell em it ain't me man. Tell em it ain't me," the cra<u>z</u>y white boy shouted. Simon was busted. He was in a corner. He hadn't done a thing, yet he was looking at serious time. Running with the wrong crowd had caught up with him, at least that's what he thought. Why not? A black man in a redneck city with a crazy white boy on drugs who's climbing in a music store to steal everything inside.

"You over there, stop!" He knew it was coming. "What you doing?" Simon had to think quickly. He did.

"I was out running. Indoor season starts in a few weeks and I've got to get ready for the meet in Columbia. That's my hometown and I want to do good in front of my family." It sounded good. Simon was wearing his track warm-up. He was lying. He could have told the truth, but would they believe him? He was looking forward to his return to Columbia. He didn't think it would work.

"Okay. Go home," the officer ordered. He couldn't believe it.

It was his second miracle. Simon should have been arrested. He did nothing wrong but there was enough circumstantial evidence to put him away. It was God's grace that allowed him to walk away. Maybe God was trying to tell Simon something.

He was called in to the police station and questioned. Eventually he told them the real story. He told them he was afraid to tell the truth that night because he didn't think they would believe him. They told him his roommates confirmed his story, and that the lady who called the police only saw one person run toward the dormitory. Simon was let go because the evidence supported him.

The crazy white boy didn't like that. He was set free on bail, and came after Simon. He had a gun. The police picked him up at the dorm after students complained that he was walking around yelling, "I'm gonna kill you, Stick!" Simon was glad when they locked him up. He should have learned a lesson. He didn't.

The only lesson he learned was to stay away from white people. He became radical black. He read the teachings of Malcolm X. After his experience, Simon was convinced Malcolm was right when he said white people were the devil. Simon forgot the white people who stood by his side during high school. He hated all white people. He forgot how Coach Pinkerton helped him when he had nowhere else to go. His anger clouded his vision.

There were others like Simon at Central Missouri State. Some were mad just to be mad. Like him, they liked getting high. Before long he was dealing on campus. Students needed weed, and he was willing to produce. He made the run to Columbia, brought weed back, sold enough to make a profit, and smoked the rest. It was a good deal, but like all good things, it had to come to an end.

Living high can get you in trouble. You're not able to think clearly while high. That's what happened to Simon. The combination of drugs and the wrong crowd ended his stay at Central Missouri State.

The conversation took place in the cafeteria. "Hey man, my cousin has a roommate who has a bad stereo. He keeps his keys under the mat. All we need to do is get the key, open the door, and take the stuff. No one will ever know," the guy said.

Simon was suckered into the scheme. After lunch they did just that. In broad daylight, they stole a stereo from a dorm room. People were watching. Everyone knew who did it.

The partner's cousin was livid. He was the fullback on the football team. He pulled Simon to the side like a brother. "Look, you return his stuff and I'll get him to not press charges. What were you thinking?" Simon was scared.

The next day Simon returned the goods. His roommates turned him in. Simon was called into the office of the President. "We have reason to believe that you were behind the theft of a student's stereo. We also have heard that you are behind the sale of drugs on campus and that you were questioned by police in connection to the break-in at the music store. You leave me no option but to expel you from school. You can continue this trimester. My hope is that you turn things around. You are a good student. You are welcome to come back next year."

It could have been worse. Simon had not taken advantage of his second chance. He returned home.

•

Simon returned home that weekend to celebrate his high school's homecoming. In a matter of weeks he would no longer be a student at Central Missouri State University. He returned home without words to share to those who hoped to see him run during that upcoming meet at the University of Missouri. How does one say, "I won't be running because I got kicked out of school"?

The football game was depressing. Simon couldn't watch. The only thing that crossed his mind was how badly he had screwed things up. If only he hadn't gotten high, if only he had stayed

away from the wrong crowd, if, if, if. The list was limitless. Simon's life could have been different, but he had no one to blame but himself. He could say it was the white man's fault. There had been many white people in his corner: teachers, coaches, and counselors. No, it wasn't their fault.

He walked around with his Central Missouri State warm-ups on. The same warm-ups he wore the night in front of the music store. Simon had taken pride in running for State, but now it was all lost. He couldn't see past that day. The thought of going back never crossed his mind. The thought of going back to college seemed impossible.

Simon walked in a daze near the concession stand when he heard, "Will you help me? Someone is harassing me. I need your help." Her name was Janet. He had met her before. Mutual friends tried to hook them up one day during lunch. It was a joke. They had nothing in common. He left thinking, what was on their minds?

"Sure. I'll help you," he said. She went on to tell Simon that an older man had attempted to rape her. He was a local minister. Simon wanted to kick his ass, but instead he walked her home. He thought nothing about it. He was simply trying to be a friend.

They shared a few words, nothing special. She lived a few blocks from the school. Once there, she invited Simon in to meet her mother. No big deal.

Her mother was drinking. "Where the Hell's Ricky? When that nigger gets home I'm gonna ground him for life." Simon chuckled. No one else did. She was a no nonsense mother. She played by the rules, and if you failed to play by her rules you

had to go. Simon stayed for a while. Excused himself, and went home.

Before long they were involved. He wasn't looking for a commitment. He was looking to pull his life back together. They were alone in her room one night. Simon hadn't made a move on her. She was tired of waiting. She told him she had never been with a man who hadn't forced her. All Simon wanted was friendship. She wanted more. They made love.

Simon soon discovered the relationship was headed nowhere, but it was too late. Simon started seeing another girl, and what he felt for her was deeper than what he felt for Janet. Janet was a great person; she simply lacked what he needed. Something was missing. Their conversations were sketchy. She didn't challenge him. Something important was missing, and Simon knew it.

Simon was tired of playing the player game. He was prepared to move on and be the man that he needed to be. For that to happen he needed to break things off with Janet. He did. He started seeing the other girl. It was early, but he felt it had the potential of going places. She was older, in college, and focused. He needed a woman to push him to the limit, not just a roll in the bed.

Simon didn't want to hurt Janet, but he knew it was the best thing for both of them. He couldn't commit to her. He didn't love her. It took him a few weeks to come to that conclusion. By the time he got there it was too late.

The phone rang. It was Janet. "I've got bad news," she said.

"What is it?"

"I'm pregnant," Simon was taken by surprise. She had informed him that she couldn't have children. She told him there was no need for him to

worry about birth control because the doctors said she would never have children. Now she was pregnant. Simon was angry. How could this happen? He would not blame her. He would not ask her to have an abortion.

"Are you okay?" Simon asked. He had to be a gentleman. Enough bad had been done. "Don't worry. I'll take care of things." He wasn't sure what that meant, but he wasn't prepared to do what he did next. He broke up with the other girl, found an apartment, and moved in with Janet. He didn't know what else to do.

Simon wanted to change his life, and if that meant doing the right thing—so be it. Little did he know that doing the right thing did not mean living together. He was only 19. He was too young to understand what a real relationship meant. He was still dealing with addiction. It was too much, too soon.

Their first apartment was a pit. They paid $109 per month, and that was too much. There were roaches and rats. The water didn't work most of the time and the stove didn't work. It was hot in the summer and cold in the winter. It was the best they could do.

Simon took a job at the hospital in food service. He helped prepare the trays for the patients. The pay was bad and the hours were long. He worked as much overtime as he could. He ran to work in the mornings and home at night. The dream of running college track was still in him. He was in good shape. He timed himself at 45.1 in the 400. He knew he had the stuff, but it wouldn't matter unless he took it to the real track.

The long hours caught up with Simon. That, along with his training schedule, resulted in a series

of illnesses. For three months he was in and out of the hospital. He became more and more frustrated with life. He sniffed cocaine to cover the pain. He needed money so he started dealing again. A little here and there from time to time to make up the difference.

The dealing stopped after he was picked up after work. The driver was waiting for him. "Hey you, hop in." It was cold and Simon needed the ride. The apartment was three miles from the hospital.

"Thanks man."

"No problem. What's your name?"

"Simon."

"My name's John. You from around here?"

"Yeh."

"Good. Maybe you can help me. I'm looking for a place to by some coke. I just moved here from Colorado, and I'm trying to set up shop in Columbia. Can you help me?"

Something wasn't right. It felt like a set up. This guy knew Simon's schedule. He was waiting for him. He was a narc.

"I ain't into none of that. I work over at the hospital. I do my job. I go home." He didn't give up. He knew Simon wasn't telling the truth.

"Come on man. You must know somebody who can help me."

"Sorry."

"Tell you what. I'll give you a piece of the action. Say I give you 15% for helping me out."

"That's nice, but I can't help you."

Simon knew then that the police were watching him. The following week the place where he brought drugs was raided. It was the biggest bust in the city's history. Simon could have been there. It was another miracle.

Simon was admitted into the hospital again. They couldn't find the cause of his problem. His legs went out on him. He couldn't feel anything. It happened after getting high. For the next three weeks, he remained locked up in a hospital room. There was no roommate. Just Simon and the walls.

Two people came to visit Simon one day. Bob Logan and his high school coach. Bob Logan was Columbia's most decorated track star. Logan had worked with Simon. He believed in Simon.

"What you gonna do when you get out of here? You need to pull it together. You have what it takes, but you have to want it Simon." Coach agreed. They knew what Simon was capable of doing. Maybe it was too late.

Simon knew the real cause of his illness. It was the drugs eating away at his body little by little. All of his dreams were being thrown out the window. The muscles in his legs were replaced with fat and bones. Gone was the stamina and grace.

His first trip after leaving the hospital was to the track. Simon tried to run. He couldn't. He collapsed after 100 yards. All of his work had been in vain. After training day after day, and building his body into a running machine, it was all gone. All he could do was cry. He didn't have the energy to try again. The dream was dead. He couldn't run anymore.

It's tough coming to grips with your past. That day Simon saw what drugs had done. Everything was lost. Nothing was left. He went to his mother's house, locked himself into his old bedroom, and had a temper tantrum. He threw things. He cussed. He cried. His life flashed before him. Everything bad done to him, and everything bad he'd done to anyone—flashed.

He threw everything in his sight. And he yelled like never before. Not at God, but at himself. "You fool! You had everything. Talent, opportunity, people behind you, and you fucked it up. You fool." He had never seen what he saw that day. "Look at what you've done. What will you do next? You fool."

His body was weak. He couldn't take any more. There was only one thing left to do. He had tried it before and it worked. He would try again. It was the only thing left. He prayed. Not on his knees, but on his face. He lay there on the floor, broken. With eyes closed and the world shut out, he prayed.

"I'm sick of me, God. I have screwed up my life, and I don't know what to do. Please take it from me. I don't know what to do with it. I don't deserve it, but give me another chance to do it right. I will not mess it up." After praying he laid there in silence. His mother and Janet were in the dining room.

Something happened. Some call it the Holy Ghost. Simon didn't know what it was. But he knew it was real. He felt God's presence. He knew God loved him. God lifted him. He cried some more, but not out of pain. It was joy.

"Thank you God. Thank you!" Simon couldn't explain it. He knew everything would get better. He was happy. For the first time in his life he praised God. Some call it salvation. No word is enough to explain what Simon felt. He knew in that brief moment that he had what it took to achieve anything. He was prepared to move forward. No more drugs, no more fighting the gift within. From that day on, things would never be the same.

•

All day Friday Simon stayed in bed reflecting on his life. As he pondered his life's critical choices, he began to wonder if any of them had been made for him. The miracles of his days were certain, yet the decisions made after each left him thinking about why he did what he did. Did he get married to prove to the world that he wasn't like other black men? Did he get married to protect himself from the cycle he had created? Did he enter ministry to prove to himself that he was worthy of God's love? Did he remain in ministry because of his desire to support people who went through life struggles similar to his own?

Simon stood at another crossroad. This time he had the power to decide what was right for him. Throughout his life he had played the look at me game. Look at me, I just finished college. Look at me; I just finished a master's degree. Hey, you, look at me, I have a Ph.D. I'm important. Look at my car. Look at my house. Look at my clothes. It never seemed to work. No matter how hard Simon worked to get people to notice-it was never enough. Something was always lacking.

That Friday, Simon had to admit that his addiction was an attempt to get people's attention. He wanted his parents to notice that he was hurting. When that didn't work he hoped that God would take notice. God had let him down, so he thought. Where was God that day when the white boys beat him the day the sun died? Where was God that day when the family friend took him on a ride to show him what it meant to be a man? Where was God that day when he asked God to heal his sister?

Simon had been waiting for God. What he failed to see was the presence of God along the way. God was there when he prayed under the tree. God

was there when the police could have arrested him. God was there when he didn't go to the house that day when everyone was arrested. God had been there. Was it enough to satisfy all the pain Simon had felt over the years?

God was there that day when Simon decided to turn his life around. The church wasn't there. No preacher was there to place holy hands and oil on his forehead, but God was there. The question for Simon was God's presence in this moment. Where was God now? Simon was angry with God again. He felt like he was at the track again. He wanted to run, but he had no strength to make it around the track. His spiritual muscles had withered due to the attack on his soul. He couldn't make it.

Simon used drugs to get the attention of those who seemed not to care. He used drugs to cover the hole in his soul. Something was needed. Nothing else seemed to work. His self-esteem was tarnished. He needed confidence. He couldn't answer any of the questions. Drugs helped him.

Simon was still an addict. His drug was the church. The problem with this new drug is it was more deadly than cocaine. It crept up behind him masked as good. It looked good. The words appeared to satisfy a deep thirst. It came cloaked as a friend. It wasn't. It was a deadly drug that had intoxicated him now to a deep despair. Could he wake up from the drudgery caused by this deceptive force? He needed a hit. He needed another amen to help him make it through the night. If someone would sing a hymn, he could make it another day. Someone please clap your hands, stomp your feet, get up and dance. Someone say "The Lord will make a way somehow." Something from the files of the holy. Anything to fix what nothing else can fix.

He hid behind the lies and deception of the church. The promises were stale. The claims of God weren't true. So much of what he had believed hadn't worked for him. He sold out to telling the same lies. The people came to make noise, but in the end of it all, their lives were just the same. They sought God yet only found their own interpretations of God. They confused the things of God with the creation of their own imagination.

Simon had sold out to the lie telling. He wanted to find God, but gave in to worshiping the church. God is found within the human spirit. He wasn't teaching them that. God isn't found between the walls we call the church, God is found within each of us. He wasn't teaching that. Simon couldn't find God for all those years because he attempted to find God using the files of the church. He couldn't find God in their sermons, or songs, or prayers, or words planned to encourage. Simon found God when he asked God to take his life. He lost God when he sold out.

Preacha' Man

Chapter Seven - Saturday

"A change has come over me"

THE BUDDHA SAYS when the pupil is ready the teacher will come. Simon was ready to be taught. He was ready for a profound teaching that brought meaning to his confusing life. After years of serving God's people he was at the point of no return. If he were to continue in his current role as the pastor of the Shady Grove Church, he'd have to buy into the life that was killing his passion, and continue to utter the half-truths God's people intended for him to speak. He could no longer force them to embrace a world of lies removed from the beauty of God's real grace and mercy. They wanted him to condemn the sinners of the world for their refusal to accept all of the lies told. To go back required the selling of his soul for a life of comfort. They would pay him to tell the lies.

He couldn't go back, but he couldn't find the strength to turn away. Why? Because beneath all the lies told, there was a truth that needed to be shared. It was the truth that helped him find himself while addicted. It's the truth of God's love and presence in the midst of the lies told, and the half-truths maintained. Simon couldn't force himself to walk away because someone had to tell

the truth. They had to be told that they were worshiping themselves rather than God. They had to be told they had replaced their interpretations of the will of God with the actual voice of God. God was speaking, yet no one stopped to listen. They couldn't hear God because they were too caught up in what they believed. Simon had to tell them, but could he?

After a long day locked up in his bedroom, Simon decided to come outside. He jumped in the shower to wash away some of the tears. Janet left on Friday morning with the kids to give Simon time alone. He thanked her then, yet wished she had been with him to help calm the voices vibrating in his head. He was alone. Jamaica wasn't there. Janet was gone. The kids were not there to take his mind off what only he could decide. He had run long enough. It was time to decide if he could continue to live as the Preacha' Man.

The hot water felt good against his aching body. Simon closed his eyes. "God, I need you to show me again. For all these years I have made decisions thinking I did it all for you. Now I know I did it for myself. Was it all in vain? Did any of it matter? Have I missed the mark? All this time I thought I was faithful. I was hurting and blamed you for my passion. All the degrees to prove myself worthy. All along looking for someone to pat me on the back. Always looking for someone to praise me — not you." It was a confession that hurt.

"How can I stand before the people knowing that I have done this for the wrong reason? Can I serve them knowing that I no longer believe what they want me to say? I feel that it is all a waste of my time. I love you God, but I hate the church."

He said it. The truth came out. Simon hated the church. He hated the people for what they had

done to him, his family, and the woman he loved. He hated the way his life was designed by them. He hated how they forced him to give, and his giving was never enough. He hated how ungrateful they were for what he had given, and for their desire to oust him despite all he had done. Simon loved God, but had a real hate for the Church.

How could he stand before them the next day? For years he stepped into the pulpit with a word that he believed came from God. He preached to people who would take his words and make them their own. They would take them out of context. They would look for errors. These people who claimed to love him and trust him were his biggest critics. They were supposed to be his family. They were to be the family of God. He believed that. He taught that. He taught people about God's love and how that love could be seen among the believers. It was a lie. There was no love in the church. They were hateful, deceptive, cruel and vindictive. They claimed to possess the spirit of God, but couldn't find love enough to lift him up in his time of need.

Simon decided to take a drive. He hoped it would help him put together a sermon for the next day. He drove until it got dark, real dark. He drove through the west and north end of the city. He drove through the east and south side. He drove looking for something, anything that could speak to his need. It was after midnight. No word from God.

He decided to take another drive by the church. Crack houses and strip clubs surrounded Shady Grove. For years, Simon attempted to move the church toward a more active community focus. They were slow to move. Many were more content with taking care of those in the pews. It all looked so familiar. Like that night when he almost

relapsed. The same faces walked the streets. The same hookers and dealers. The same pain and struggle. Nothing had changed, there was just more of it.

It hurt Simon that so much needed to be done; yet the church was more concerned about his sex life and rumors. He wondered what would happen if the energy that went into crucifying him was placed on cleaning up the neighborhood. It all seemed like a waste of time. It was all a lie. The thing that mattered wasn't being done, and the thing that mattered the least became the subject of debate.

He stopped at the stoplight on the corner of Main Street and Harrison Avenue. "Hey, you want to party," a hooker knocked on his window. "Can I get a ride?"

Simon was amused. The woman was ugly and fat. She was missing most of her teeth. He thought of the good old days when the hookers looked good. These contemporary hookers made it hard to be tempted. He chuckled, but offered to give her a ride. What the heck, he thought. I'll give her $20 and tell her to go home. He knew it wouldn't work. She would take the money, buy some crack, and head back to the streets. Hookers had interesting stories. They knew what was going on in the streets. Simon liked keeping in tune with the life of the streets. It gave him an edge.

"What's your name baby?" Simon knew not to give her his real name. That would ruin the game.

"Jeffery. What's your name?"

"They call me B.J. You want to know why?" she licked her lips.

"You so nasty," Simon laughed.

"You the police, baby?" they always asked that question.

"No! Do I look like the police? Have you ever seen a cop as fine as me?" He was having fun. "Are you the police? That's the question."

"You know any police that can lick their lips like me?" she responded by licking her lips again. "So what you want, boyfriend."

"I want to go home, take a shower and go to bed."

"You want to take me with you"

"No thanks. I'm not that desperate. I like my dick, and if I'd fuck you it might fall off. I need two dozen rubbers to protect me from that shit."

"No you didn't! Then what you pick me up for motherfucker?"

"I felt sorry for you. I'm your social worker tonight and I decided to bless you with some food stamps," Simon pulled out a $20 bill and handed it to her.

"That' fine with me. Pull over at the next corner."

"Not yet. You tell me your story. Tell me your story and I'll give you another $20 and then both of us take our ass home."

"Why you want that?"

"Because I get turned on talking to freaks and hookers," he said. "Now, I ain't no fool. If you down I'm getting the fuck out of this neighborhood. You look like a woman who has a mug shot on file, and I'm not going down like that. I'm driving to the north side. After you tell me your story I give you $20 and take your ass home. That's $40 bucks and you don't have to suck no dick." It was Simon's way of ministering to the hookers. Sometimes it worked and women turned their lives around. Other times they fed him a line of bull. In a strange way, it satisfied his urge to walk on the wild side.

"Tell me how you got started in the business."

"Because I needed the money," she was being evasive.

"You know what I mean. What was it that put you over the edge."

"I needed the money, and I like the sex." That was different.

"You're telling me you like your work. You got to be kidding. With all of these diseases and crazy men out here."

"Some of them treat you nice. A couple of them feel in love. Mostly truck drivers. My regulars are cool with me. They watch after me."

"So, you're telling me you did it because you wanted sex?"

"No, I did it for the money and part of the reason I keep doing it is because of the sex. Shit, ain't that hard. Who else you know can make $20 in five minuets?"

"You got it going on like that?"

"Most men can't handle the heat."

"Why this instead of another job?"

"A person got to do what you got to do. I tried to get other work, but I ain't got no GED. Most of the jobs don't pay enough and I need my money. And, I can't pass the test.

"What test?"

"The drug test."

"So you using? What drug?"

"Cocaine."

"Crack?"

"Yep."

"You ever tried rehab?"

"Three times."

"You ever thought about going back?"

"There ain't no rehab no more."

"I understand. I know the game. I'm a recovering addict."

"Must be nice to be clean."

"It takes one day at a time."

"That's what they say."

"You want to know my secret?" Simon wanted to help. He needed to help. This was what ministry meant to him.

"What?"

"You have to know your trigger. You have to know the thing that pushes you to the edge. You know what I mean? When you hear the pipe calling your name and the next thing you know you're taking your mamma's TV to the pawnshop. You need to know what drove you to that point. You ever been there?"

"Hell yes! I wake up in a cold sweat the damn dream is so bad. I keep saying I ain't gonna use. The next thing I know I'm on the corner, or stealing somebody's shit."

"The thing that helps me is to figure out what's going on in my mind when that happens," Simon went on. "For me it was the death of my sister. After she died I didn't want to live no more. I wanted to die. I used to cover the pain. My trigger was feeling alone."

"I know that's right. I know my trigger."

"What is it?"

"God." In all his years in working with addicts it was the first time he heard one say that.

"What you mean?"

"You know that church back there. The big one. Shady Grove. I used to be a member there. I grew up in the church. I used to sing in the choir. I loved going to church. That was until I was 10."

"What happened?"

"You want to know. I never told nobody. My moms don't even know why I don't go no more. She still go there. She loves the pastor. She keeps talking about how he can help me and shit. I ain't studying that church or the pastor. They can all kiss my ass," B.J. sounded like she was ready to cry. Simon understood. He wanted to cry.

"Why do you feel that way?"

"Because I got screwed by God. When I was 10, I stayed late one night after Vacation Bible School to play with my friends. It was getting dark and I had to get home. We don't live far from the church so walking was easy. Moms told us we could stay out as long as we made it home before the street lights came on."

"Your moms sounds like mine. She would beat me if I came home after the street lights came on."

"That's my mom. Anyway. One of the deacons told me he had something to give my moms. He taught my class sometimes. I went inside to see what he had. He locked the door. He started touching me. I tried to run, but he grabbed me," she paused. Simon let her take her time. "He raped me right there in the church."

She was raped at about the same age that Simon wrestled in the truck. He understood her pain. Like him, she was raped by a person she trusted, a deacon in the church. One called to serve the people raped one of the innocent babes. Simon was ready to fight.

"What did you do next?" he asked.

"I didn't do anything. No one would believe me."

Simon had to know. "What was his name? I have to know." Simon stopped the car and held the

194

hand of the woman hooked on crack because of God.

"You believe me?" she asked.

"I believe you. I'll tell you why. When I was a little boy about the same age as you were then, a man took me on a ride in a truck. He took me on a dirt road. He told me he was taking me home from school. He took me out in the middle of nowhere and made me suck his dick. I told no one. I was hurt, and because of that, I used too. Do you hear me? I've been there. I believe you, and I want to help you. I don't think God did this to you. An evil man did. He was not God. He pretended to be."

"You don't think God did this to me?"

"No."

"Why would God let it happen?"

"I don't know the answer to that. I wish I did. I wish I had an easy answer, but if I gave you one I'd be lying to you. I don't know why God didn't stop what happened to you, and I don't know why God didn't stop what happened to me. But, I know one thing, God is a miracle worker. You know how I know? Because I'm talking to you. I needed to see you tonight. I needed to hear from God. Do you know who I am?"

"No."

"Would you like to know?"

"I know you a good man."

Simon closed his eyes and thanked God. "I'm the pastor your moms told you about. God sent me to you tonight, and God sent you to me. Tonight you have ministered to my spirit, and God is telling you to go back home. Things will be better there. You'll see."

"Deacon Andrews," she blurted. "His name was Deacon Andrews. Go get him for me."

Simon was reminded of the text from Ephesians, "Take no part in the unfruitful works of darkness, but instead expose them. For it is a shame even to speak of the things that they do in secret; but when anything is exposed by the light it becomes visible, for anything that becomes visible is light. Awake, O sleeper, and arise from the dead, and Christ shall give you light." He now understood the text. For the past few weeks he kept turning to it. He thought it was about him. Now he knew what it meant.

"No B.J., bullshit, what's your real name?"

"Carmen."

"Now that's really special. My daughter's name is Carmen. This is how we're going to do it, Carmen. We're going to get him together. Tomorrow, oops, today. We're going to expose him together, and we're going to pull your life back together.

Chapter Eight - SABBATH

"When you've done all that you can, stand"

FOR THE FIRST TIME in a long time, Simon walked in the church with a smile on his face. The people expected him to be downtrodden after Thursday's meeting. He laughed and joked with the ministers before the worship service like his old self. Simon was known for his sense of humor. It was back.

The church was packed as usual. On this day many came to see the fireworks display. The word of the meeting had spread through the city and many people came to view the chaos. It was a wonderful day.

Many of the 45 stayed away in protest. Simon didn't mind. The thought of not having them there was a wonderful thing. All he cared about was one thing. He wanted to make sure Deacon Andrews was there. He was. He had already regrouped for the next round. The word of the separation had spread. Andrews was planning to use it to stir up more opposition. "Good luck Andrews. You might get 46 the next time," Simon said under his breath as the choir sang.

The choir was on fire. Many of Simon's supporters were in the choir and they praised God for the victory. Despite the victory, Shady Grove was still a church divided. Simon knew it. Knowing it made it easier for him to do what he planned. He bowed to pray. It was time to preach. "God this is your word. Take it. Use it. Amen." Short and simple. He was confident.

There was a hush when he stood.

"As always, this is the day the Lord has made, and we shall rejoice and be glad in it. We shall rejoice from the pews and the choir stands. We shall rejoice from the pulpit and deacon row. We shall rejoice from the sanctuary and the streets of the city. Let everything that has breath praise the Lord," he began.

"Amen," was heard around the church.

"This week has provided me the usual circumstance of having to wait on the Lord until the last moment. I was not sure if there would be a need for me to preach today, and even in my knowing I was not sure as to what to preach.

"As always I trusted that God would provide the right words for the day. I depended on God to give a word that lifted and inspired the dejected while piercing the souls of the guilty. I have sought God to give a word that wasn't too much of me, yet helped me grow. Yes, I needed to preach to myself. Sometimes, a preacher has to do that. Sometimes you're so low that the only thing that can help is to preach to your own pain.

"I found these words from Paul's Epistle to the Church at Ephesus. It's the 5th chapter the 11-14 verse. 'Take no part in the unfruitful works of darkness, but instead expose them. For it is a shame even to speak of the things that they do in secret; but when anything is exposed by the light it becomes

visible, for anything that becomes visible is light. Awake, O sleeper, and arise from the dead, and Christ shall give you light.'

"Before I help you today, I have to make a confession. My confession should not shock you, for if you were to tell the truth, you would be forced to make the same confession. Paul's word startled me. This word brought to the forefront the agonizing truth of my life. A part of me has been asleep. No, it's worse than that. A part of me died a long time ago.

"Someone's thinking, what you talking about, preacher? I'm talking about having been cradled to sleep in the process of the doing. Some have slept so long without knowing it. They're sleep walkers. The snore of their slumber has become so overwhelming that it looks like death. No one recognizes this condition. You can get by. The sleepwalkers of the world are able to exist in this false state of existence. Why? Because everybody else is sleeping. No one is awake. All of us have been hypnotized by the forces of evil to a state of rest. We walk, but sleep. We talk, but sleep. We inhale and exhale, yet sleep. We think, yet sleep.

"How do I know there's death? When there's more Hell in the church than there is in the streets—that's sleep. When we witness the decline of a community, yet a larger church building being erected to house God's people—that's sleep. When we note a change in the economic status of a few, yet zombies walk down the street—that's sleep. When we have men and women in our church who have been raped by its leadership—that's sleep. When we have young girls selling their body for one more hit of crack—that's sleep. When we have young people dropping out of school and church folk acting a

fool—that's sleep. When we have more talk about who does what, and no talk of what we must do—that's sleep. We have fallen asleep, and the stench of death is in the air. The church is in a coma. You may not want to say amen, but you know I'm right about it.

"How did we get there? What is it that caused this deep snooze? I'm glad you asked. We fell asleep, first and foremost because we've hidden behind a mask. We have lived under a façade for so long that we don't know our own names. We have lived to satisfy other people without considering our own desire. We have built a life to please people we don't know or like. Who are you now? Who are you when the mask goes off? Paul talks about the light. When we read these words we assume it's a word for those outside the church. It's for those people who don't do right. For those people who have not accepted Christ in their life. Paul is writing to a divided Church. On the one end of the spectrum were the Jewish Christians. On the other were the Greek believers. The age-old struggle of the faith community has been to find a way to speak to the variety of voices in the midst.

"We sleep because we try a cookie cutter approach. We rob people of their true identity. We tell them what it means to be a Christian and then judge them when they fail to fit the mold. This is the way you should wear your hair. This is the way you shout. This is the way you clap. We don't do that at this church. We pray this way. God says you should read the scripture standing up. Oh, you have to speak in tongues before you can be a real member. We'll accept you as a provisional member, but you're not ready yet. We need to see your bank statement to assure that you pay what you really are

to pay in tithes. This is what it means. Fit in or be in the judgment of God.

"We sleep because we lie. We lie because we don't always feel like saying praise the Lord. Sometimes I don't feel like praying, but I can't tell you that. I can't because I have to act the way you want me to act or stand in judgment of the people of God.

"We sleep because we hide. We hide behind our houses and degrees. We hide behind the things we're told define a good Christian. A good Christian does these things; we tell them. They run around attempting to be something they're not able to be. They end up in debt, depressed, confused, and angry because we told them this is what it means. They're asleep.

We sleep because we fear the light. That's the second reason. Paul tells us that things done in the dark should be brought to the light. Expose it. Don't be scared of the light. The light will help you. The light isn't your foe. The light is your friend. Don't hide from the light. It will heal you. It will inspire you.

We fear transparency. That's why we sleep. We fear people getting to see the real person behind the façade created. We can't tell the truth. We can't say we're hurting. We can't let the people see us cry. We can't tell a person when we've made a mistake. Why? Because if we do it becomes the subject of public discussion.

"You and I have been rocked asleep by our continuing to live the lie. There's no place to go. The light is shining, but no one can go to make a confession. No one can say, 'I need the light.' Instead we pretend that we have the light. We pretend we're awake. We're not. We're asleep.

"How do I know? Because darkness causes a person to look at others instead of considering their own ways. Darkness points the finger over there instead of looking over here. Darkness says, 'They need help,' rather than, 'I need help'. You stay there because so much energy has been spent looking at others that you failed to see your own need. Too much time looking for stuff in other people's eyes. Too much time trying to find reason to condemn others.

"I've learned an important lesson. Paul helped me with it. I learned that I have too much to deal with on my own to consider someone over there. If I get caught up in identifying their issues, I may, in the process, miss out on my own deliverance. We're asleep because we fear the light. We fear what they will see. We fear what they will do with what they will see.

"Who's to blame here? I hate to tell you this. I have to tell the truth. It's the fault of church people. What happened to creating a place where people can feel comfortable with telling the truth? What happened to no hiding place? What happened to the loving, caring community of God that lifts up those so low they can't get up on their own? What happened to the loving caring community that acknowledged all have sinned and fallen short of the glory of God? What happened to the caring community that listened to testimonies and handed inspiration instead of condemnation? You and I are asleep today because the church is no longer the church. It has become a club with membership requirements, oath and initiation rites, rather than a hospital for weary souls who come just as they are.

"But that's not the only reason. We also sleep because we're comfortable walking among the dead. Paul challenges the church to wake up. He tells

them to rise from the dead. He's telling them—he's telling you and me—to get out of the graveyard. Stop being a tomb dweller. Embrace life, not death. Get out of the grave of despair. Wake up! Get out of the grave of self-doubt. Wake up! Get out of the grave of guilt and shame. Wake up! Get out of the grave of deception and greed. Wake up! Get out of the grave of put downs and keep them down. Wake up! Get out of the grave of I can't make it cause I'm black. Wake up! Get out of the grave of it's always been this way. Wake up! Wake up! Wake up! I said get on your feet and stop walking among the dead, depressed, negative-minded, hard-headed, stony heart, and bruised minds of the grave. Wake up and claim yourself today. Get up and walk out of the grave and embrace the light.

"Look at the light. It's shining over there. Can you see it? Paul tells us he was blinded by the light. He had to be blinded before he could see. Why? Because he only saw with a human eye. He was blinded so he could see from the inside out, instead of the outside in. Can you see the light? Be careful. You may go blind first. Blinded of your will over the will of God. Blinded of what you think. Blinded of what you get out of it. Blinded of your tricks and schemes, and opinions, and desires, and what you think God wants life to be. You'll be stripped first. You'll be humbled first. That's what the light will do. But oh, thanks be to God, after it's all over. After the blinding is over, God will open your eyes. And like me, you can sing, 'My eyes have seen the glory of the coming of the Lord.'

Wake up! Wake up! Wake up! I was asleep. I've been rocked to sleep by the church. Rocked to sleep by what you thought I should be. But I'm awake now. Thank God my eyes have been open.

Thank God I can see again. Thank God I have my life back, and this joy that I have, the world didn't give it, and the world can't take it away.

"I'm sorry to tell you that the church didn't help me get there. God got me there in a different way. I didn't get there by listening to the hymns and the sermons. No that couldn't help me no more. Your high praise and the sound of the organ didn't help me. No, no. The holy dance didn't help me get there. No, no. Your amens and handclaps couldn't help me. No, no. So, you may wonder how I got there. How is it that God woke me up?"

"Excuse me! Excuse me; I've got to speak! I have to speak!" It was Carmen making her way to the front of the church.

"Young lady, you are out of order. I'm in the middle of my sermon." Simon looked frustrated and angry at the suggestion.

"I have to speak. You said things need to be brought to the light. I have to bring something to the light. I can't take it no more. God won't let me rest."

"Do you have to do it now? You're interrupting our service."

"I'm sorry. I have to. I've been holdin' it in for a long time. I have to tell it today."

"Let the woman speak brother pastor. The spirit must have moved," said Deacon Andrews, approaching. "Let the woman speak."

"Thank you. I'm standing because you said things need to be brought to the light. Something happened to me, and I have to bring it to the light."

"Go ahead sister," Andrews coached her along as he touched her shoulder.

"I was raped by someone in this church. It really hurt me. You talked about people being raped by people in the church. I think God was

speaking to me when ya said that. I can't rest no more. I been hurting for a long time. I'm telling you now because someone else might get hurt. God help me. He's got to be stopped."

"You say this person is a leader of the church?" Andrews asked.

"Yes."

"Is this a high ranking leader of the church?"

"Yes."

"Is he here today?"

"Yes."

"Can we all see him right now?"

"Yes." The people feared the worse. Simon bowed his head as if guilty of a crime. He took his seat and placed his head in his hands as to weep. Deacon Andrews noticed. This was the end he'd been waiting for.

"You're right honey. It does need to be exposed. We can't allow this kind of thing to happen to you. You tell us who it is and we'll contact the authorities to arrest him. He'll be punished. We stand for justice. Now, who is it?"

Carmen took his hand off her shoulder. She looked him in the eye. "You don't remember. You don't remember when you asked me to come into the church to take something home to my mother? You don't remember closing the door and locking it and raping me on the church floor? You don't remember me? Why would you? I was only 10 then. I haven't been back to the church since you raped me. I thought God did it to me. My mother told me to come back after I got hooked on crack. I started using because of you. I got so bad that I sold my body to support my habit. I did that for a long time. That was until I met the pastor of this church. He helped me out. I'll be all right, because I've seen

the light. Like the pastor, my eyes have seen the glory of the Lord. My life won't be the same no more, but you stand in God's judgment for what you did to me. I ain't scared no more, Deacon Andrews, you no good child molester."

Andrews stood frozen before the people. Carmen would not move, the years of waiting and hurting had come to an end. Simon stood and picked up his Bible. The crowd was silent. What was next? What do you say? Simon stood in front of Andrews. Close enough to kiss.

"The word of God reads, 'You, therefore, have no excuse, you who pass judgment on someone else, for at whatever point you judge the other, you are condemning yourself, because you who pass judgment do the same thing.' You said one thing that is true Calvin Andrews. We do stand for justice at Shady Grove. The authorities will be called. Deacons, take this former deacon to his seat.

"I thank God for Carmen's courage," Simon continued as he held her hand. "We have a lot in common. She is my friend. The Buddha says, when the pupil is ready, the teacher will come. God has a way of sending teachers in strange places. They don't always come in the pulpit. Sometimes they preach from the corner. Many times they don't even know they're being used by God. I'm asking that you promise to love Carmen. She's been away for a long time. She loves God, and God loves her. God has a work to do through her. I want you to promise me because I won't be around to watch over her. Promise me you won't judge her for her past. It's not all her fault. Some of the blame is sitting over there. What I'm trying to tell you is, I have to leave the church to save my own soul. I can't find my peace in the church. I can't hear God the way I need to in the church. I can't be free to be

me, in the church. So, today is my last sermon. Don't worry about me. I'm awake now. My soul is at peace. My life is in God's hands. I'm free to be me."

The crowd roared in disapproval. Even the 45 present seemed to have changed their minds. Simon could see the guilt on their faces. Sophie cried. He smiled her way letting her know he cared. No hard feelings. No need to cry.

"Remember this as I prepare to go to Jamaica, our struggle is not against flesh and blood, but against rulers, against the authorities, against the powers of this dark world and against the spiritual forces of evil in heavenly realms. Therefore, my brothers and sisters, put on the full armor of God, so that when the day of evil comes you may be able to stand your ground, and after you have done everything to stand, stand."

Simon walked out the back for the last time. He never looked back. The Preacha' Man was free to be a man. There was only one thing on his mind. Find Jamaica.

ACKNOWLEDGMENTS

I am indebted to those who read the book before it went to press: Greg Hardy, Janice Webster, Detreecia Byers, Leandra Hines, Tonya Redd, Joyce Jenkins, Katina Rankin, Brett Chambers, Beverly Mahone, Rhea Norwood, Valerie Chestnut, and Betty Redwood Davis. My appreciation and gratitude to them and all those who helped me garner the courage to press forward. This has been an act of faith.

My gratitude to Anita Daniels for loving me when I was ready to give up. You have a special place in my heart.

To Kathy Kenney for marrying me when I was too young to know any better and staying with me despite my imperfections.

To Prinn Deavens, my best friend, for proving that men and women can be just friends. Someday, I pray, you will be my best man.

Thanks to Glenda Jones for proving that love can happen again, but when it comes, be sure you are ready. If people only knew the real you.

Thanks to the Herald-Sun in Durham, North Carolina for trusting me enough to write a column each week. To the many who read my column. You've helped me grow.

Thanks to Dr. Harmon Smith who taught me ethics at Duke University the Divinity School. You gave me the confidence to write. To the late Alan Neely who stood in my corner. Cleo LaRue, J. Randall Nichols, and the rest of the faculty at the Princeton Theological Seminary. I will never be the same.

To the members of the Orange Grove Missionary Baptist Church, for watching me grow

up and loving me enough to say it's time to go. You did me a favor.

To the partners of Compassion Ministries of Durham for loving me for who I am, and giving me the space to cry and breathe. I see God in you.

Dedicated with love to Carl and Doris Kenney, my parents; Felandus, Lenise and Krista, my children; Julian, their little brother; Sandra, my sister; Andre and Sharonda, my nephew and niece. Reverend Robert C. Scott, my soul brother. Carl Washington, my big brother. I miss you man. You died too soon.

ISBN 141202483-8